MW01593914

Double Play

Art Voellinger

"I dreamed of being Babe Ruth or Joe DiMaggio."

iUniverse LLC
Bloomington

DOUBLE PLAY

iUniverse books may be ordered through booksellers or by contacting:

iUniverse
1663 Liberty Drive
Bloomington, IN 47403
www.iuniverse.com
1-800-Authors (1-800-288-4677)

ISBN: 978-1-4917-0084-6 (sc)
ISBN: 978-1-4917-0086-0 (hc)
ISBN: 978-1-4917-0085-3 (e)

Library of Congress Control Number: 2013913368

Printed in the United States of America.

iUniverse rev. date: 09/06/2013

Chapter 1

The 11 p.m. to 7 a.m. (graveyard) shift at the Stag Brewery in Ashville, Illinois, offered Frank Slade many options during the winter of 1958. Regardless of his duties, he could dream at work after establishing himself as a valued employee since being hired by the Griesedieck Western Brewing Company in 1945.

After returning from World War II, he became versatile. Recognized as a former baseball player at Ashville High School, where many considered him among the city's best ever, he also was admired as a filler operator or an uncaser, packer, or release person for any of the jobs along the conveyer line.

As he watched Stag beer poured into 72 bottles per minute during a Thursday night shift in mid-March, he enjoyed the freedom of musing. Meanwhile, a five-inch snowfall reminded Ashville that winter lingered.

Times were good. In Ashville, a guy could make close to three dollars an hour and get by even if he had a wife and three kids. For Slade, security had increased in 1954 when the Carling Brewing Co., of Cleveland, Ohio, purchased the assets of the Griesedieck Western and added Stag to the Carling product line.

Carling also owned the Hyde Park Brewery in nearby St. Louis, Missouri, but when the latter closed, Ashville expanded its capacity to 1.4 million barrels per year. By then, Slade and 200 other employees were familiar with everything from brew kettles, to storage tanks, to bottle lines, to racking facilities for draft beer.

Known in the Ashville area as the Stag Brewery because that beer had been brewed there since 1912, the company location was easily identified by the word STAG, painted in vertical, white letters on the brewery's smokestack. The landmark represented the 13th largest brewery in the United States.

By '58, Carling had added Black Label and Red Cap Ale to its Ashville production, with the former benefiting from the recognition gained from radio and television commercials featuring a bar customer requesting a beer by saying, "Hey Mabel, Black Label!"

Whenever a fellow worker sang the jingle during a shift, Slade remained his usual quiet self while keeping a keen eye out for misplaced labels or improperly filled bottles. He also refused commenting on employee T-shirts featuring the Stag label (in red) beneath a brown male deer's head and above the word BEER (in brown). On the back, words expressed: "Brag about Ashville and Stag."

Ironically, Slade had a huge thirst for beer 15 years earlier while fighting for his life as an Army Sergeant in the Ruhr Valley in Germany. The World War II Battle for the Ruhr marked the final defeat of the German Army and was in the past as was the Korean War, which he had avoided due to his age and having a family.

In '58, peace prevailed across the United States, and Slade preferred concentrating on the spring and another season of playing men's amateur baseball for the Champion's Sporting Goods team of Ashville. Seated near rows of twisting and turning bottles, he recalled the 1953 season when the Champs captured the St. Clair County League regular season and playoff championships. After dethroning perennial power Freeburg in the playoffs, the Champs' players and fans acted as if they had won the World Series of Major League baseball.

"Champs Claim St. Clair Crown" exclaimed the banner headline of the *Ashville News* sports page Slade kept along with a team photo given to each player by Edward Champion, the sporting goods store owner.

Memories, though, lacked more Champs' titles due to Freeburg's return to dominance. Individually, Slade, at age 37, was a graying senior citizen at third base. If aging dwindled his talents, he was about to experience other changes. Men home from military service were improving the caliber of the St. Clair League and sparking rumors about a merger with the Monroe County League.

While on the job, seated at a table in the brewery's lunch room, or when driving home in his 1948 Chevrolet Fleetwood station wagon, Slade let baseball dominate his thoughts. As he steered his weathered, mahogany-paneled vehicle into the carport of his simple, white, frame home on South Second Street in Ashville, he had no concept of the thoughts annoying his wife Kathy.

Chapter 2

After 13 years of marriage, 37-year-old Kathy Ellis Slade preserved the beauty, warmth, and class that had attracted Slade. For her, as early as their senior year in high school, she had developed feelings for the 6-foot-2, lanky three-sport athlete. Not only was he tall and handsome, she considered him one of the nicest guys a girl could meet. As students, they became familiar with one another as a result of his playing sports and her being a cheerleader. They became friends after Kathy, against the will of her parents, asked Slade to the school's annual Sadie Hawkins dance.

Academically, if he struggled, she was eager to solve a math problem or explain the significance of a historical event. Likewise, whether at school or on a date, he was mannerly, and enjoyed being with her, especially if he could do something as educational as defining a baseball term. As recently as 1957, after she had won tickets to the Municipal Opera in St. Louis where she dragged him to watch *Damn Yankees*, he proudly explained how being a power hitter meant "being able to hit doubles, triples, and home runs."

More impressive was his knowing why the "Shoeless Joe from Hannibal, Mo." referred to in the stage production was not the Shoeless Joe Jackson of the Chicago Black Sox.

"I read about the real Shoeless Joe in a *Sport* magazine somebody gave me at work," Slade said. "He was part of the Chicago Black Sox Major League scandal in the early 1900s."

For the high school sweethearts, love in the 1940s was no different than in any previous era. Sometimes the explanation could be found in the eyes of those involved, but in the case of Kathy and Slade, how they treated each other was a sign of a potential marriage.

Their wedding occurred shortly after Slade returned from the war, and was not looked upon as unusual by Ashville citizenry other than William "Bill" Ellis, Kathy's father, who demanded they get married.

Although a parent of two daughters, Ashville National Bank executive Ellis took special pride in Kathy's sister Carol. A high school valedictorian, Carol had taken a position as a secretary at an Ashville law firm where she met a young attorney. After they married, they moved to the affluent St. Louis suburb of Ladue and settled into high society.

For Kathy, four years younger than her sister, her father's pride had been tested and tarnished.

The war and Slade's Army service delayed their thoughts of marriage and forced her to live at home with her parents. Thanks to her dad, after she graduated from high school, she worked as a teller at Ashville National where the elder Ellis could readily observe his beautiful, brown-eyed, sandy-haired daughter.

However, things changed drastically in 1944 after Slade came home on leave, and she became pregnant.

"No daughter of mine is going to disgrace my family like this," were words that echoed for Kathy.

Nonetheless, "Bill," as he was known in the banking community, wanted to keep the pregnancy private. In Ashville, he was as successful at that as trying to predict when the war would end, or how long it would take to rejuvenate the economy.

"As soon as he's discharged, you get married and get the hell out of my house," Ellis had shouted, assuming that neither his wife nor Kathy would take exception.

"And you damn well better tell that SOB I don't care how many Nazis he kills, he's no friend of mine."

Representative of a family that thrived on work and its financial rewards, Bill Ellis advanced from bookkeeper to bank executive in a fashion similar to his father, who climbed from being a postal clerk to an assistant postmaster. Both men carried a confidence linked to when the first generation of the Ellis family came from Germany to the United States and settled in the Ashville area.

Often, Kathy and other family members heard of great grandpa William (formerly Wilhelm) Ellis. A coal miner, he conveniently shortened his last name from von Schultzenheimer to Ellis, as in Ellis Island, which greeted the immigrants in New York Bay. Unfortunately, the Ellis great grandparents and grandparents were long deceased before Kathy gave birth to daughter Kate - named in recognition of grandmother Kathleen, who had lived with her husband on a small farm outside of Ashville.

After Kate's birth and Slade's discharge from the Army, Kathy's father maintained a cool attitude toward his son-in-law and added insult by saying, "I'm glad it was a baby girl; at least she looks like her mother."

The newlyweds disregarded negativity by moving into the vacated home of Slade's Aunt Mary, two blocks from the memorial fountain in downtown Ashville. Raised by Mary in the absence of parents who died during a flu epidemic in the early 30s, Slade also was indebted to Mary, whose death led to his inheriting the property.

To Bill Ellis, Kathy's home was inferior to his brick, ranch-style home in Chenot Place. Named after Augustus Chenot, who emigrated from France to the U.S. in the late 1830s, Chenot Place represented a class level Augustus' father, Jean Joseph Chenot, achieved as a personal body guard for Napoleon Bonaparte.

While the Bill Ellis home reflected the comfort and recognition a bank executive deserved, Kathy resided in a 50-year-old cramped, one-bath home with two small bedrooms upstairs and one in the basement. Repeatedly told by her dad that she could have done better by marrying the son of a doctor or lawyer or any of the Country Club set in west Ashville, Kathy enjoyed her post-war environment with Slade, especially after their surprise of 1951 - the birth of twin boys.

Now, seven years later, as Slade returned from work on a Friday morning, he anticipated being with his family. He knew his children,

Kate, an eight-grader, and Jim and John, first graders, would be home due to a teachers' meeting.

After stomping his feet to dislodge snow from his shoes, he entered the kitchen where his senses were struck by more than the smell of coffee and sight of a breakfast of bacon and eggs. On the corner of a Formica table lay a copy of *Woman's Day* magazine, and from an area in front of the kitchen stove, Kathy turned and said, "We need to talk."

Chapter 3

Considered quiet by some and a loner by others, Slade was different when he was with Kathy. From the first time they met, he could speak openly, and on this morning, after sharing a hello kiss, he was not initially concerned with her request.

"One of the kids in trouble?" he asked after placing his car keys, a half-empty pack of cigarettes, and a lighter on the table.

"No, they're fine and sleeping," she said while placing food on their plates and a coffee pot on the table.

"Then, what's up?" he asked.

"Frank, it's time we make a better life for our family," she said.

Accustomed to coming home, eating, and then sleeping after his wife and kids departed for school, Slade took a bite of food, sat up straight in his metal legged chair, and hesitated to respond as he glanced at the cover of *Woman's Day*.

"Coffee tastes good, bacon and eggs are good, I've got a steady job, we've got a roof over our heads, and the kids are doing okay in school," he said.

"Frank, there's much more to life," she said in a tone more in line with a consideration than a challenge and befitting her roles as wife, mother, and home maker.

"What's this all about, Kathy?" he asked. "You been reading crap in that magazine, or did your old man put you up to something?"

"Oh, come on, Frank," she said. "The magazine has more recipes than personal advice for women, and my dad really does care. After all, we have his only grandchildren.

Despite not wanting to argue about Ellis, Slade commented on the '48 station wagon that had been a gift from Ellis.

"If he cared so much, he should have given us the fancy Cadillac he's driving instead of the 10-year-old clunker that replaced my beat up Chevy," said Slade, who often referred to his father-in-law as "Mr. Ellis."

"Frank, when dad bought the station wagon, he thought it was a good idea," Kathy said. "It had room for things like his dogs, or plants for his garden, or fishing equipment. And after our kids got bigger, he knew we'd have more use for it."

"You know I don't like getting anything from him; I kept my mouth shut because of you," Slade replied before asking, "Is this about money?"

"You're already working part time at the grade school cafeteria" he added. "That's helped us pay for some things, but these kids need you here."

"Frank, I'm not talking just about money, and I'm not disagreeing about the kids," she said. "After all, Kate is almost in high school, and the boys are going to get involved in sports. But I need to get out of the house and see what's going on in the rest of the world."

"They're opening a Kresge's Five and Dime across the street from the Lincoln Theater in town, and Betty, one of the other cooks at the grade school, said I'd be ideal at the lunch counter. From what she said, it would just be on Saturdays."

Realizing that his wife's working would mean he'd have to assume more responsibility at home, Slade wondered if he had entered a give-and-take proposition.

If he said, "Yes," his wife might consider herself too demanding or him too easy. If he responded, "No," he knew she could take exception. Again, he stared at the cover of *Woman's Day*. While waiting to reply, he heard the basement door open, and realized the conversation with his wife may have been overheard.

From the stairwell adjoining the kitchen, Kate emerged. Dressed in worn pajamas and slippers, she stepped toward the table, bent over, hugged her dad, and asked her mom, "Did you tell him how we want to make this his best baseball season ever?"

Chapter 4

Whether influenced by the presence of his daughter or the realization that women were part of the work force at the Stag Brewery, Slade agreed to Kathy interviewing at Kresge's.

"It would give you a change of scenery," he said.

After waiting nearly a week to understand how his wife and Kate could aid his baseball skills, Slade focused on possible self improvement.

"If beer could be pasteurized to eliminate bacteria," he thought, "what could improve a 37-year-old batter's swing?"

During the '53 season, he learned about techniques used by Joe Schmidt, a renowned Ashville native who hit .441 in 1939 for the St. Louis Cardinals' Class D team in Duluth, Minnesota.

According to Champs' manager Red Morrison, Schmidt would take a new Louisville Slugger and shave the bat handle with the broken neck of a Coca-Cola bottle to make the bat easier to grip. Morrison also told Slade of how Schmidt tempered a bat.

"Joe said it was not unusual for him and some of his teammates to build a fire with wood chips outside their home park dugout, put rosin on their bats, and then rotate them in the fire," Morrison had said. "That would bring the grains on the bat closer together and make it more compact."

The recipient of a silver-plated bat for his efforts in '39, Schmidt played 14 seasons in the minor leagues. Despite a career batting average of .324, he never reached the major leagues.

For Slade, hitting .300 or higher was something he experienced from the time he starred at Ashville High School. But after '53, his average and power declined.

Was it due to age or having put on weight? Or, was it the result of his right knee and an occasional popping sound when he walked? Originally jarred when he jumped into a foxhole in Germany, the knee received little attention from Slade until he twisted it one night while turning in a chair at the brewery. Aspirin had been a remedy in '53, but the drug's affect on inflammation could not guarantee a high batting average.

As he watched rows of Stag beer bottles at work, Slade wondered if using a lighter bat would improve his hitting. His decision could be aided at Champion's where the Champs received a discount when making a purchase.

At Champion's, he would be able to select from rows of Louisville Sluggers and Adirondack Co. bats, but this year he faced a dilemma. He could continue to swing a Louisville bat of the same dimensions, like the one used by Detroit Tigers' Hall of Famer Hank Greenberg, or purchase an Adirondack model made famous by players like New York's Bobby Thomson of the Giants and Mickey Mantle of the Yankees.

According to a *Sport* magazine advertisement, Adirondack was about to market a northern white ash bat with "Flame Treated" etched on the barrel. Would Slade choose a bat similar to one used by Greenberg or one influenced by Schmidt's techniques?

His choice would not be based only on the recognition of Greenberg being the first Jewish star of professional sports in the United States. The Detroit home run hitter (58 in 1938) also was the first American League player drafted into World War II, and the first pro baseball player to re-enlist in the military after the bombing of Pearl Harbor.

Bat selection could be a challenge, but Slade encountered a different concern when he took an early-morning, coffee break in the brewery's lunch room. Upon entering, he found two teenage boys seated at a table and another standing and filling plastic cups with beer poured from a tap in the wall.

The spigot holder, who Slade recognized as the star halfback of the Ashville High School football team also was a son of one of the brewery's executives. In brash fashion, he stood and raised a cup as if to salute Slade, whose reply of "What in the hell are you guys doing in here?" brought curious looks.

Obviously, the boys enjoyed having access to the room where the Stag employees routinely could taste one of their products. Now, the boys' conclusion to Friday night frolicking and free beer had been discovered.

"Say hello to the great Frank Slade," the halfback said in a slurred, mocking tone to his friends.

"The greatest three-sport athletes in the history of Ashville High, but not good enough to play pro baseball."

Pierced by the appraisal, Slade calmly poured a cup of coffee, took a seat at an opposite end of the table, and stared back at the threesome.

Impacted by the stare that could have been taken for a glare and by Slade's 220-pound frame, the boys gulped their beers and moved quickly to a side exit. En route, their spokesman offered a one-finger gesture that spoke volumes for a generation influenced by the likes of James Dean and Elvis Presley.

"Smart ass," Slade muttered as he finished his coffee. Later, he could reconsider his bat choice in an environment where surprises of a lesser nature came in the form of a stopped conveyer or a broken beer bottle.

Chapter 5

Driving home from the Stag Brewery on a Saturday morning was convenient for Slade because his '48 Chevy was reliable. No need to dwell on the car's faded red color or worn side panels during a 20-minute drive. After reaching home, he could anticipate the day's activities his wife regularly outlined via a note on the kitchen table. On this morning, he also would go to Champion's to purchase a bat.

A harbinger of spring, the late March sunlight erased remnants of earlier snow falls and forced Slade to roll down the driver's side window, breathe deeply, and think of baseball. As he hummed along with a popular Perry Como song, he applied the lyrics to himself rather than to the intended love interest.

"Catch a falling star and put it in your pocket, never let it fade away!" caused Slade to ask himself if he were a falling star in baseball.

His musing also kept him from appreciating the song's advice: "For when your troubles start multiplyin', and they just might! It's easy to forget them without tryin', with just a pocketful of starlight!"

Coincidentally, after the recent incident in the brewery lunch room, he justifiably could have wondered if his troubles were increasing as he came to a sudden stop in the carport.

"What in God's name is that?" he groused while turning off the ignition key. After stepping from the car, he approached what appeared

"Could a single have as much impact as a home run?"

"*One Home Run* is more than a baseball story. A clever blend of fact and fiction, it features the influence of chance encounters and is a pleasant reminder of a bygone era when the game served as a centerpiece in the fabric of life in small-town America."

—Gary Mueller, retired sportswriter, St. Louis Post-Dispatch

"*One Home Run* is not just an enjoyable read with memorable characters, but a lesson in accepting the growing pains of becoming an adult. An enticing baseball metaphor for life, it sparks youthful memories and seductive reveries of a time when life was simple, but emotions were complicated."

—Judee Sauget, producer, Zingraff Motion Pictures

"From base to base, *One Home Run* carries the imagination of anyone who has played baseball or wanted to play the game. Along the way, it offers life lessons."

—Bud Zipfel, former Major League Baseball player

HARD COVER,
SOFT COVER,
Q-book AT

AMAZON.COM

ISBN 978-1-4620-1068-4

90000

Art Voellinger
236 Warrensburg Dr.
Belleville, IL 62223-3437
VOELLINGER01@AOL.COM

9 781462 010684

to be a green Army blanket hung in such a way that it blocked the car's path.

Pushing the blanket aside, he found more surprises. Standing in the center of the carport was an object which would have been more discernible had it not been for another Army blanket hanging from a clothes line and blocking sunlight from the rear.

Closer observation revealed what he recognized as the inflatable Joe Palooka punching bag he gave his sons at Christmas. The gift had been meant to introduce them to boxing and self defense.

"Boys need to be boys," he had told his wife of the 32-inch high, rubbery, plastic bag.

Marketed as a "Joe Palooka Bop Bag," the dummy, in the likeness of the popular blond comic strip character, stood above a sand base. Throw a punch into the face of heavyweight champion Joe, depicted in a boxing stance with gloves extended, and the bag would drop backwards and then recoil to an upright position.

Unlike at Christmas, when the boys took their first and only turns striking the bag in the living room, Palooka stood taller. Contributing to his height were two rows of magazines placed side by side as a perch for the sand base.

Had Slade examined closer, he would have spotted copies of "*Woman's Day*," but he became distracted when Kathy emerged from the side door of the carport.

"What's this for?" he asked as his wife approached carrying a baseball bat.

"Just watch," she said while placing a box filled with worn tennis balls near the bag.

Next, she put a tennis ball on top of the bag where a slight indention conveniently permitted three-fourths of the ball to be exposed. Then, after mimicking a batter's stance, she swung the bat through the ball that sailed against the blanket at the rear of the carport.

"Here, give it a try," she said without disclosing details of previous attempts when she smashed Joe Palooka's nose.

Eager to outdo his wife, Slade grabbed the bat, took two practice swings, placed another ball atop the bag, and hit a line drive directly at the blanket. However, the ensuing loud pop was not the only noise of consequence. From behind the door leading to the kitchen, applause erupted from the three Slade children. Their smiles reflected knowledge of their mom's experiment and delight in its success.

"You can adjust the height of your swing by placing more magazines under the bag," Kathy said.

"If I don't swing too low, Joe should hold up until spring," said Slade, whose hugs of his wife and children advanced his plans to purchase a bat.

Chapter 6

The fourth Saturday of March 1958 and its afternoon temperature of 55 degrees allowed Slade to decline his wife's offer to join her and their three children for a visit to the kids' grandparents.

By refusing a ride to Champion's, he could use the two-mile walk as exercise while anticipating what bat he would find for the approaching baseball season. Hopefully, it would be as durable as the model he used the previous season and during the past two weekends when he experimented with his carport batting tee.

Carrying the 35-inch, 34-ounce bat on his right shoulder, he walked toward downtown Ashville like Paul Bunyan with lumber on his mind. At the Square, so named because of the buildings that formed a square around the city's war memorial fountain and circular thoroughfare, he was greeted by a fellow brewery worker in front of the city's only pool hall.

"Hope you do better with your bat than I did with my cue stick," the worker said.

"I'm not so sure hitting a baseball is easier than stroking a cue ball," said Slade in an attempt to stress the difficulty of playing the popular Ashville pool game called "3-5-and-8."

At a corner of East Main Street, he directed his attention to Champion's, some three blocks away, where an ambulance was parked on the sidewalk in front of the store. Increasing his pace, he crossed the street and approached a curious crowd. When he reached the edge of the group, he understood why some observers stood on tiptoes as attendants placed a stretcher into the rear of the ambulance.

"It's Edward Champion," one bystander said.

Unable to see if the victim actually was the store owner, Slade stood near the entrance and became convinced of the observer's accuracy when he heard Johnny Champion's voice.

"I'll follow you to the hospital," said the owner's son as the ambulance driver activated the vehicle's siren to clear a path to the street.

Resting the barrel of his bat on the pavement, Slade watched a clerk change a sign in the front door from "Open" to "Closed" and listened as the crowd dispersed.

"Somebody said Johnny found his dad slumped over his desk," said one man to another. "It must have been a heart attack."

Regardless of their accounts, Slade knew if the attack were fatal, Johnny had been groomed to succeed. In recent years, the owner's only child emerged as more than a subtle influence. At age 26, he controlled everything from display windows to newspaper advertising. His merchandising methods included emphasizing the need for baseball batting helmets from youth to adult leagues, especially after a 1956 major league rule required the wearing of helmets or protective plastic liners under the baseball cap.

The relationship between safety and sales convinced Slade that Johnny would maintain Champion's quality reputation in the southwestern Illinois area and continue to support the men's baseball team. As he walked home, Slade kept the bat off his shoulder, spoke to no one, and recalled Edwards Champion and the '53 team's playoff title, clinched on a crucial play involving Johnny.

Normally the team's scorekeeper, Johnny entered the game in the ninth inning as a left fielder after two Champs' players (shortstop and left fielder) were injured in a collision trying to catch a fly ball. Despite having a handicapped left arm as the result of a childhood injury, Johnny came to the plate for his first ever at-bat.

With an Indiana college kid named Randy Wilson at third base, Johnny faced overwhelming odds against Freeburg's highly-touted pitcher. However, when Johnny leaned away from an inside fastball, he made enough check-swing contact as a right-handed batter to send a fly ball down the right-field line. The opposing second baseman made the catch, but failed to prevent Wilson from sliding in with the winning run.

For Slade, the 4-3 victory was part of a daydream snapped by the reality of his wife's approach in their driveway.

"Red Morrison just phoned; Mr. Champion is dead," she said.

After embracing his wife, Slade spoke of the morning's events, which had become the fodder of Ashville phone lines. As they entered their house, he returned his bat to its home.

Chapter 7

The largest cathedral in Illinois, St. Peter's Cathedral, with its lofty spires, flying buttresses, and large stained glass windows, provided a striking spiritual character for Ashville's downtown area. The seat of the Diocese of Ashville, the cathedral served an estimated 1,000 parishioners and others living in the southwestern Illinois area.

Consecrated in 1887, the church was nearly destroyed by fire in 1912 but rebuilt and modeled in the English Gothic style after the Cathedral of Exeter, England. In 1956, the brick walls were refaced with Winona, Minnesota, split face dolomite (mineral form of calcium magnesium carbonate) and trimmed with Indiana limestone.

On Saturday, March 29, 1958, the cathedral became the site of the noon Mass of Christian burial of Edward Champion. During the previous two nights, long lines of visitors viewed the sporting goods store owner at the Renner and Sons Funeral Home where Johnny Champion stood alongside his uncle, prominent Macon, Georgia, attorney Earl Champion, Earl's wife Ann, and their 24-year-old daughter Georgia Ann Champion.

At the cathedral, where purple Lenten decor hinted of Easter Sunday, the Champions sat in a front row pew with Johnny. While the latter seemed somber and tired from two nights at Renner's, the visitors seemed relaxed and conditioned for the praise worthy of a civic leader and friend of the church. After the casket was placed a few feet from the first pews, Monsignor Patrick O'Donnell, pastor of the Cathedral parish, officiated in a fashion designed to make the funeral a celebration of life.

After providing personal facts about Edward Champion, whose wife had died in a car accident a few years earlier, O'Donnell expressed condolences to Johnny and the rest of the Champions. The Monsignor then recalled how Edward, a 63-year-old native of Ashville, gave his home town a family business reflective of a lifelong work ethic.

"How fitting for a champion of business, civic, and charitable organizations to display similar zeal as the sponsor of a men's baseball team called the Champs," said O'Donnell, who was assisted in the Latin language Mass by Father William Grace Martin.

Currently the pastor at a church in Chicago, Father Martin was known as Billy Grace in '53 when he lent his left-handed pitching to the Champs' late-season run. In a break from funeral tradition, he also was the lead pallbearer of a group including Walter Irish, the *Ashville News* sports editor; Dutch Schmidt, owner of the Foul Ball Tavern across the street from the Athletic Field, home park of the Champs; Red Morrison, the team's manager, and former player Kent Keller, who, in the championship game, had struck out preceding Johnny Champion's crucial fly ball.

Slade, whose height and broad shoulders made him more prominent to the large church audience, was the last pallbearer and stood behind the casket.

Originally opposed to the baseball interests of Father Martin, O'Donnell said Edward Champion's sincerity and an offer to allow the Monsignor to sit with him at the Athletic Field contributed to "a welcomed summer diversion."

"Baseball has a way of bringing people together," said O'Donnell as Slade, Irish and Schmidt exchanged looks, knowing the Monsignor had received a financial contribution from the sporting goods executive.

"We go now to Mount Carmel where we will bless Edward Champion a final time, hoping all of us will never lose our memory of a life fulfilled."

"Dominus vobiscum," said the Monsignor, meaning "The Lord be with you," and leading to a response of "Et cum spiritu tuo," meaning "And with your spirit."

During the drive from the church to the cemetery near the end of Ashville's long West Main Street, Schmidt wondered aloud if Edward Champion's death would affect the sponsorship of the team.

At a post-funeral luncheon at the Dutch Girl restaurant, any doubts were put to rest. Johnny Champion already had informed Morrison and Irish of intentions to take over his father's business and increase support of the team that would face new challenges in the form of reported league expansion.

Chapter 8

Traditionally, the Saturday before Easter abounds with the Christian anticipation of Christ's resurrection. For Slade, the anticipated purchase of a baseball bat became more significant than heavenly issues.

"Can I improve my batting average with a better bat?" he asked himself.

His wife could select the best Easter outfits for their children. His goal was to find a bat capable of enduring the games and weeks of another season.

After dropping Kathy and the kids off at Kresge's where she had successfully interviewed and would learn her schedule, Slade parked his station wagon in front of Champion's. Inside, he met Johnny Champion, whose work place in a loft at the rear of the store provided a view of all visitors.

"Things getting back to normal?" Slade asked.

"About as good as can be expected," Johnny said while directing Slade to a bat rack and barrel containing Louisville Sluggers.

"35-inch, 34-ounce," said Johnny. "I haven't forgotten."

"That's me" Slade replied. "But this year I also want to look at some of those Adirondacks."

While pointing to another bat rack, Johnny explained how the Adirondack Co. was promoting the wood of their bats made in Dolgeville, New York.

"They've placed "Northern White Ash" in script above the Adirondack label," Johnny said before changing subjects.

"I assume you read in Irish's column about a St. Clair League meeting a week from Sunday at the Foul Ball.

"I want you and Red (Morrison) there with me," Johnny said. "I spoke with Irish and Red, and phoned some of the other managers. Itt sounds like the St. Clair and Monroe teams might merge."

"From what I gathered, Lee Mathews (St. Clair League president) already has met with Bill Moore (Monroe League president). They may form two divisions, but I guess we'll still be playing Freeburg, Marissa, New Athens, Lebanon, Mascoutah, O'Fallon, and St. Libory."

"What about the new Ashville team?" Slade asked. "There are rumors Les Mueller will sponsor it."

Recognized for years for having pitched 19 2/3 innings as the starting pitcher for Detroit in a 1945 Major League game against the Philadelphia Athletics, Mueller had taken over managing his father's furniture store in Ashville but never lost his zest for baseball.

"He pitched for the Tigers in the ('45) World Series against the Chicago Cubs," Johnny said. "The last few years when he wasn't pitching with Johnny's Tavern down by South Side Park, he'd also play corkball.

"Irish said some teams from the St. Clair League might disband, but he thinks Tilden, which is near Marissa, might join the new league. He said Moore wants to form another division, including Millstadt, which is in St. Clair County, but played for years in the Monroe League. Millstadt is closer geographically to Waterloo, Valmeyer and Columbia."

No longer stationed at the front desk of Champion's, Johnny savored being a leader. At 5-foot-6, he did not possess the physical stature of his father, but his direct tone allowed Slade to appreciate the maturity and transition Edward Champion had envisioned.

After Johnny graduated from high school, the elder Champion insisted his son attend nearby McKendree College in Lebanon. The school's location allowed Johnny to commute, earn a business degree, and stay close to the family store.

"Dad respected you," Johnny told Slade. "He always thought you were good enough to play pro ball. Pick out the bat you want, but tell the kid up front to apply the team discount."

"Damn nice of you," said Slade as Johnny stepped toward the stairs leading to his office.

"Find a good one," Johnny said. "Make Dad proud. I'll see you at the meeting."

Chapter 9

I n 1905, future Hall of Famer Honus Wagner, the star shortstop of the Pittsburgh Pirates, signed a contract with the Hillerich & Bradsby Co., manufacturer of Louisville Slugger baseball bats. The first pro athlete to endorse a retail product, he also was the first player to have his autograph displayed on a bat.

After playing for the lowly Louisville, Kentucky, Colonels of the National League, he joined the Pirates in 1900 and won the first of his eight batting titles.

Slade, an avid reader of sports publications, learned of Wagner's endorsement in a feature story in the St. Louis based *The Sporting News*. However, in selecting his own Louisville model, the Ashville slugger was influenced by more recent players.

Among the National League batting champions endorsing Louisville Sluggers were Stan Musial of St. Louis in 1957, Henry Aaron of Milwaukee in '56, and Richie Ashburn of Philadelphia in '55.

As Slade organized his carport batting cage, he recalled reading how Ty Cobb referred to a baseball bat as "a wondrous weapon," and smiled at the thought of Ashburn. The Phillies' center fielder reportedly said, "To cure a batting slump, I took my bat to bed with me because I wanted to know my bat a little better."

On a Saturday morning, Slade intended to get to know his new bat in a different way while recalling more about Ashburn and the 1957 season. According to an *Ashville News* wire story, Ashburn, a left-handed batter, did something that may never be duplicated in baseball.

On Aug. 17, 1957, he hit a foul ball into the right-field stands at Connie Mack Stadium in Philadelphia and broke the nose of a female spectator. Amazingly, during the same at-bat against the New York Giants, he hit another foul ball toward the grandstands and struck the same woman in the chest as she was being taken out of the stadium on a stretcher. Adding to the uniqueness of the events was that the woman, Alice Roth, was the wife of *Philadelphia Bulletin* sports editor Earl Roth.

Unlike the spray hitting Ashburn, who had 2,579 hits during a 15-year Major League career but only 29 home runs, Slade was never a batting champ. In the St. Clair League, many of his blasts were caught in baseball parks lacking an outfield fence.

In his carport, an Army blanket made the catches and survived better than Joe Palooka's head, which suffered whenever Slade struck the lower half of the tennis balls.

Dressed in sweat pants, sweat shirt, and tennis shoes, Slade ripped line drives, drawing cheers from a chorus of three - his daughter and twin sons. And, after each smash, either Jim or John would retrieve a ball while the other placed a different one on top of Palooka.

After the boys had positioned themselves atop empty beer cases near Kate, who sat on the top step leading into the house, Slade re-established his right-handed stance and swung.

"Holy Cow!" yelled Kate into her clenched right fist, which served as an imaginary microphone as she mimicked popular Cardinals' radio announcer Harry Caray. "It might be . . . it could be . . . it is! A home run," she said. "Listen to this crowd."

Energized by the ensuing applause, Slade gripped his bat tighter, but this time hit under a ball to such a degree that it flew into the carport ceiling.

"He popped it up!" said Kate with extra emphasis on the word popped.

"Where'd you learn that?" Slade asked, not knowing how Kate often turned her radio dial to Cardinals' broadcasts after hearing complaints about the volume of her favorite rock and roll music.

"Who doesn't like baseball?" Kate asked before hearing an offer from her dad as he removed the magazines from beneath the inflated bag.

"Here, take a couple swings, but be sure to choke up on the bat handle," he said.

As her brothers watched in awe, Kate swung and hit line drive after line drive, bringing cheers from the boys and praise from Slade, who produced another surprise for all three children.

Reaching into a duffle bag, he pulled out three white, light-weight, plastic perforated balls, two youth size, yellow plastic bats, and a black, rubber batting tee—all items Johnny Champion had received from a Connecticut manufacturer promoting a game called Wiffle Ball.

In the back yard, for the remainder of the morning, Slade and Kate taught the boys how to adjust the tee and hit off it. After a successful swing, each boy would run in an imaginary base path, allowing Kate to embellish in Caray style. The boys' achievements thus became stories to share with Kathy Slade after her return from Kresge's.

For Slade, additional stories were on the horizon in the form of the St. Clair League meeting.

Chapter 10

The April 13 meeting at the Foul Ball tavern brought together Slade, Red Morrison, and Johnny Champion, and representatives of teams from the counties of St. Clair and Monroe. Chaired by Lee Mathews, the meeting was meant to combine the teams of the two longtime leagues and establish the best level of men's amateur baseball in southwestern Illinois.

By arriving an hour early, the Champs' threesome thought they could use the time to contemplate roster and uniform/equipment needs for the 1958 season. But after being interrupted by sports editor Walter Irish, their intentions yielded to his insight and a few beers.

"You guys will have trouble against some of those Monroe teams" Irish said. "You already have your hands full with Freeburg in your own league, and teams like Waterloo, Millstadt and Valmeyer won't make it any easier."

"They aren't new to us," Morrison said. "We've played them in practice games for years."

"That may be true," Irish said, "but practice is just that, and I know them from watching the Valmeyer tournament."

Accomplished with a microphone as well as with a typewriter, the 64-year-old Irish had served as the public address announcer at St. Clair all-star games played at the Ashville Athletic Field and as a master of ceremonies at the league's annual winter banquet. In 1957, he was asked to help with the play-by-play of the July Fourth weekend tournament in Valmeyer where he could expand his talents.

"It's their way of getting publicity and my way of being able to announce while reporting on the tournament," said Irish, who relayed information about the Monroe teams and their leaders.

"Waterloo will kick your ass, and rub it in every chance they get," said Irish. "Those players are like their manager. He wants to win at all costs, and goes out of his way to recruit players. He's also a tight ass. From what I heard, he puts whitewash on worn balls and reuses them in games."

Irish's tale brought a smile from Champion and a raised eyebrow from Slade before Morrison added more. "We've played them a few times at their ball park and at ours, and the way they hit home runs, it didn't matter what kind of balls were used," said the 67-year-old manager.

After indicating that Slade also was capable of hitting home runs over the fences at Waterloo where the ballpark sat on a plateau, Irish referred to Millstadt where that team's diamond had no fences and featured a grandstand less than 30 feet from home plate.

"Step into the batter's box there, and you can hear everything from the spectators' conversations to each time a beer can is opened," said Irish as Dutch Schmidt placed drinks in front of his guests.

"I know you play Millstadt for a half barrel before every season, but they play hard with or without a bet," Irish said before taking a sip of Stag beer and adding a beer-related story.

"They also like to party, and after they upset Waterloo two years ago for the championship, they met at a tavern in town. The place has an outdoor beer garden and a screened-in porch where people from all over the area go to eat chicken or fish on weekends.

"Anyway, after Millstadt won, they gathered outside to celebrate when one of the players thought he'd add to the excitement by tossing a bucket of water on their manager - the guy they call Tuffy.

"To get away from the player, Tuffy ran toward the porch. When he got inside, the player was close behind and close to a St. Louis couple eating near the screen door. That's where the player, in an attempt to douse Tuffy, missed and hit the woman smack in the head.

"All hell could have broken loose because the woman was in shock after her black, bee hive hairdo melted and hung down around her face. Fortunately, after Tuffy stopped, and the player stopped, the woman's husband broke out laughing to break the tension. From what I heard, the woman, after accepting apologies, was more upset with her husband's laugh than the water."

Hopeful of continuing with stories about Valmeyer, Irish was interrupted by a familiar voice.

"Irish, you spreading more of your bullshit?" asked Mathews, whose entrance to the Foul Ball indicated meeting time was near.

Chapter 11

A longtime resident of New Athens, Lee Mathews, like others attending the meeting, had played baseball in his youth and after high school. As a catcher, a foundry worker, or a league official, his size aided easy recognition.

Often, when attending a St. Clair League game, he'd pull his black, Buick Roadmaster within a reasonable distance from a field, open the driver's side door, and remain in the front seat while observing the action. At the Foul Ball, after taking his 300-pound bulk to a table, he lifted a metal chair off the wooden floor as if to check for the chair's stability.

Shortly thereafter, Bill Moore joined Mathews. A former manager at Waterloo, Moore had moved to Ashville to work at a printing company where he was able to publish schedules and flyers at a reduced cost for the Monroe teams.

The merger of the leagues though would not be based solely on convenience or costs. Those facts became obvious after Mathews and Moore revealed winter discussions and agreeing on a league name, constitution, and bylaws. Mathews would serve as the league president and Moore as vice-president. St. Libory postmaster Norm Sutter, a longtime St. Clair secretary-treasurer, would remain in that position with the new league.

"We have an opportunity to put together the best men's amateur baseball league in the Midwest," said Mathews, confirming what Walter Irish had written.

"We're going to call it the Greater County League because the league will include teams from counties other than St. Clair and Monroe," Mathews said. "We'll retain St. Clair and Monroe as the names of the divisions out of respect for the history of those leagues, but that does not mean a team is located in one of those counties."

While Johnny Champion and Red Morrison were seated with representatives of 13 other teams, Irish and Slade sat at a nearby table and were eager to hear about everything from divisional alignments to schedules.

According to Moore, the St. Clair Division would have two Ashville teams, the Champs and Mueller Furniture, and teams from Freeburg, Mascoutah, O'Fallon, St. Libory, and Tilden. The Monroe Division would include Waterloo, Valmeyer, Columbia, Chester, Millstadt, Fults, and Dupo.

"That's 14 teams with seven in each division," Moore said. "We can compete with anybody in the Inter City League or in St. Louis," he said.

Mathews' reference to counties was supported by the placement of Millstadt in the Monroe Division with Chester from Randolph County. New to the St. Clair Division with Mueller Furniture was Tilden from Randolph County.

While Les Mueller, the player-manager of the Mueller team, was well known, Tilden manager Tom Kirk was of a lower profile but respected.

"Don't take him lightly," Irish told Slade. "He's whipped teams in the Coal Belt League in southern Illinois, and now, with Marissa and New Athens not fielding teams, he's got a huge area to find players."

Located five miles from Marissa and 14 miles south of New Athens on Illinois Route 13, Tilden, population 625, boasted a baseball diamond in a park and a tavern where Kirk tended bar whenever he was not away on a baseball mission.

"From what I've heard, he's a heck of a recruiter," Irish said. "He also collects money for his team although he once faced questions after a woman in Carbondale was a repeat winner of the shotgun he raffled."

More important to Slade was the sports editor's tale of New Athens native Whitey Herzog playing in the St. Clair League before signing as a 17-year-old outfielder with the New York Yankees in 1949. Herzog eventually reached the major leagues with Washington in 1956.

Irish also spoke of Marissa native Warren Hacker pitching for Cincinnati and Philadelphia in 1957, and pointed to the high school level where Arlie Smith at Marissa, and Larry Stahl at New Athens, both pitcher-outfielders, attracted pro scouts.

"They're left-handed hitters with power, but Larry's only a junior, and he's something special," said Irish, whose reference to prospects stirred thoughts of what might have been for Slade.

After recalling personal achievements during sips of beer, Slade paid attention to the meeting that closed with Mathews' reminders. Moore would print and distribute schedules of the Sunday afternoon games; the league season would begin on Mothers' Day, May 11, and home teams would be required to pay the umpires $2.50 each per game.

While some managers took the opportunity to schedule non-league games, Johnny Champion made an agreement with Mueller that would affect the Champs' schedule and personal plans for Slade and Irish.

"He agreed to take our place for games during the July Fourth weekend at the Athletic Field," Johnny told Irish, Morrison and Slade. "We're going to Valmeyer."

"You guys will love that tournament," Irish said.

"When's the first practice?" Slade asked Morrison.

Chapter 12

Like any of Ashville's 28,000 citizens in 1958, Slade found the warmth of spring a welcomed boost to his passion for the game of baseball, which flourished under the title of "National Pastime."

As a World War II veteran, he knew the game's popularity became enhanced when United States President Franklin D. Roosevelt sent his famous "green light" letter to Major League Commissioner Kenesaw M. Landis.

On January 15, 1942, with the country at war, Roosevelt re-emphasized the meaning of national pastime when he wrote in part: "I honestly feel that it would be best for the country to keep baseball going. There will be fewer people unemployed, and everybody will work longer hours and harder than ever before."

"And that means that they ought to have a chance for recreation and for taking their minds off their work even more than before.

"Baseball provides a recreation which does not last over two hours or two hours and a half, and which can be got for very little cost. And, incidentally, I hope that night games can be extended because it gives an opportunity to the day shift to see a game occasionally."

As far back as 1856, writers of the *New York Sun* used the terms "national pastime" or "national game" in reference to baseball.

In Ashville, the first hint of spring was not the first robin. More poignant was the *News* headline exclaiming, "Baseball Season is Here!" Optimism prevailed, and with the St. Louis Cardinals opening at home on April 15 against the Chicago Cubs, writers like Walter Irish could be excused for having fun with the game and its language.

In his "Irish Brew" column, he referred to an essay penned by 18th century English poet Alexander Pope, who may not have known a baseball from a billiard ball. According to Irish, Pope's "An Essay on Man" began with: "Hope springs eternal in the human breast," and concluded with: "The soul, uneasy and confin'd from home, Rests and expatiates in a life to come."

To Irish, the essay meant that no matter the circumstances, man always hoped for the best. Apply that interpretation to baseball, and a 20th century journalist like Irish could incorporate a play on words while informing readers that "at the start of a new season, hope especially springs eternal for Major League teams and players."

"There are no winners, no losers, no leaders, no streaks or slumps until after the first pitch of the spring," he proclaimed before stressing that baseball is a game.

"When I hear a big leaguer refer to a game being a battle, I cringe," he wrote. "The only real battles were in places like Normandy and Iwo Jima."

On a lighter side, he pointed to New York Yankees manager Casey Stengel, whose language was called "Stengelese." After noting that Stengel had been married in Ashville in 1924 while a member of the Brooklyn Dodgers and during a series in St. Louis, Irish wrote: "I hope his bride could understand him."

Among the quotes attributed to Stengel were: "I don't like them fellas who drive in two runs and let in three." "Good pitching will always stop good hitting and vice versa," and, "When a fielder gets a pitcher into trouble, the pitcher has to get out of a slump he isn't in."

An official scorekeeper for the St. Louis Browns before they moved to Baltimore in 1954, Irish closed with a quote by former Browns' owner Bill Veeck, who said: "Baseball is almost the only orderly thing in a very unorderly world. If you get three strikes, even the best lawyer in the world cannot get you off."

For Slade, humor existed outside sports pages. On a Saturday morning after his wife had gone to Kresge's, his daughter Kate displayed wit.

When emulating Harry Caray during her dad's carport hitting became repetitious, broadcaster Kate provided variety with a commercial interruption. In a voice similar to television's Dinah Shore, who sang, "See the USA in your Chevrolet," Kate improvised.

"Make a date today to see Frank Slade hit away," she sang. "He's the greatest dad of all."

For father, daughter, and sons who watched and listened, hope and love had sprung eternal.

Chapter 13

Although Greater County League president Lee Mathews believed the new league could be the best in the Midwest, he knew competition existed on both sides of the Mississippi River. Among the notables were the St. Louis and East St. Louis Muny Leagues, which had developed numerous major leaguers, and the two-state Tandy (Negro) League, including the East St. Louis Colts, and Brooklyn, Illinois, Robins.

Boasting Illinois teams only, the Inter City League stretched nearly 50 miles from Pocahontas to East St. Louis, which had three entrants. Also involved were teams from Alton, Collinsville, and Granite City.

East St. Louis topped the talent development in the form of 1957 World Series players, pitcher Bob Turley, and outfielder Hank Bauer of the New York Yankees. However, the veteran leader for the '57 Series champion Milwaukee Braves was second baseman Red Schoendienst of Germantown, Illinois. Also a member of the 1946 Series winning St. Louis Cardinals, Schoendienst was traded to the New York Giants in 1956. The Giants sent him to the Braves on June 15 of '57. As a teenager, he earned scout scrutiny while honing his skills in the Clinton County League, whose teams occasionally opposed teams from the St. Clair and Monroe leagues.

In '58, southwestern Illinois high school and Junior and Senior American Legion levels of baseball continued to generate interest, but the amateur teams remained secondary to Cardinals' mania. No longer part of a two-team Major League baseball city, the Cardinals maintained a large Midwest radio network boosted by the 50,000 watts of St Louis KMOX. Also invaluable were broadcasters Harry Caray, Jack Buck, and Joe Garagiola.

In Ashville, Slade, via a pocket transistor radio at work, was among the enthusiastic listeners of the Cardinals' opener against the Chicago Cubs. The game offered another opportunity to wear a Cardinals' ball cap and envision himself as one of the players, especially one with Illinois roots.

Cal Neeman, the Cubs' starting catcher, was a native of Valmeyer. He graduated from Dupo High School and played basketball and baseball at Illinois Wesleyan College in Bloomington before signing with the Yankees. The Chicago pitching staff included right-hander Glenn Hobbie, a native of Witt, Illinois, and the Cardinals' roster listed infielder Dick Schofield of Springfield, Illinois.

The 5-foot-9, 155-pound Schofield became the Cards' first bonus baby. He signed for an estimated $65,000 in 1953, the year August A. Busch purchased the team and changed the name of Sportsman's Park to Busch Stadium. Sought by 14 of the 16 Major League teams, the switch-hitting Schofield made his debut at age 18 on July 3 of '53. He was one of a group of players paid $4,000 or more and required to be on a big league roster for two full seasons.

Another Cardinal at the start of the '58 season was right-handed pitcher Von McDaniel. A year earlier at age 17, he received a $50,000 bonus after graduating from Arnett, Oklahoma, High School. In his first start, he notched a 2-0, two-hit victory over defending National League champion Brooklyn en route to a 7-5 record and a 3.22 earned run average.

Regardless of the year, Slade remained tormented by never being offered a professional contract. Often, he wondered what made the players of the 1950s any better than he was when he graduated from high school in 1940 as the area's most feared hitter.

For the strapping 6-foot-2, 190-pound Neeman, playing before the largest night-game crowd (26,246) in St. Louis history became memorable. In the ninth inning, he hit a towering home run down the left-field line to complete a 4-0 victory. Although the game featured future Hall of Famers, Ernie Banks for the Cubs, and Stan Musial for the Cardinals, Neeman hit the only homer - a disappointment to fans wanting to see the Anheuser-Busch scoreboard's eagle flap its neon wings after a Cardinal home run.

"I knew I hit it well," Neeman said. "My only concern was if it would stay fair," he added of his first of 12 homers in '58.

The blast came off Cardinals' left-hander Tom Flanigan, who relieved in the ninth inning for his only National League appearance before being sent to the minor leagues where he completed his career. According to Bob Burnes, the sports columnist of the *St. Louis Globe Democrat*, Flanigan joined the ranks of one-game pitching wonders but did better than former Cardinals' pitcher Willis Koenigsmark. A native of Waterloo, Illinois, Koenigsmark faced three Brooklyn batters on September 10, 1919, when he allowed a base on balls and two hits and two runs and was returned to the minor leagues.

Against the Cubs, Musial captured national headlines with a single to place him in a tie with retired New York Giants' star Mel Ott for the National League career hit lead at 2,876.

Absent from radio and newspaper reports before and after the game was mention that in 1950 at Joplin, Missouri, of the Class C Western Association, Neeman had been a Yankees' teammate of Mickey Mantle. By '58, Mantle already was a two-time reigning American League Most Valuable Player.

Coincidentally, in 1949, Mantle played for Independence, Kansas, of the Class D Kansas-Oklahoma-Missouri League, which included former Freeburg players, infielder-outfielder Charlie Weber with Independence, and infielder Kent Pflasterer with Chanute, Kansas. In '47, the KOM included Bill McFarland, a first baseman from East St. Louis, with Independence, and Jack Nesbit, a catcher from Ashville, with the Pittsburg, Kansas, Browns.

The 17-year-old Mantle played in his first pro game on June 14, 1949. Batting seventh and playing shortstop, he went 2-for-5 with two singles in a 13-2 victory at Chanute. Weber, batting second and playing right field, was 1-for-5 with a single. For Chanute, Pflasterer, batting third and playing shortstop, was 3-for-4 with two singles and a double.

Of the players involved, only Mantle reached the major leagues, making his debut in 1951. On April 16, 1957, Neeman debuted with the Cubs, who had obtained him from the Yankees in December of '56 in the Rule 5 draft.

In a Walter Irish column recognizing southwestern Illinois and its baseball roots, Neeman's name appeared alongside others with Major League experience. Also mentioned were Ashville's Norm Schlueter and Bob Groom, and former East St. Louis prep standouts, Ed Blake and Sam Jethroe.

Groom pitched a no-hitter for the Browns against the Chicago White Sox in 1917, and later coached the first American Legion youth baseball team in Ashville in 1939. Schlueter caught for the White Sox in 1938 and '39 and for Cleveland in '44, and became the Ashville Legion team's coach in 1955.

Blake, a right-handed pitcher, appeared in the big leagues with Cincinnati (1951-53) and Kansas City (1957). He was acquired by KC from Toronto of the Class AAA International League where he had been a teammate of outfielder Jethroe, who played previously for the Boston Braves and Pittsburgh in the National League.

Adding to Slade's anguish was an April 14 wire service story about Ashville native Bob Goalby edging Sam Snead for the Greensboro, North Carolina, professional golf tournament title. In addition to crediting Goalby, 27, for winning his first major title and $2,000, the Associated Press referred to the versatile athlete as an outstanding high school catcher who had ignored pro baseball offers.

Spurred by the AP's recognition, Irish again used literary allusion and wrote: "When it comes to producing great athletes, change Ashville's name, and it would not matter. For instance, if called Oakville, in respect of something other than an ash tree, or Belleville, due to having the beauty of a belle, the city would smell as sweet."

Even if Slade had read Shakespeare's *Romeo and Juliet*, and the line, "a rose by any other name would smell as sweet," he continued to wonder.

"Were these guys all better than me?" he asked himself while recalling how, as an amateur, he often saw his name in sports page headlines.

Chapter 14

Baseball seasons do not begin with the first pitch or sound of a bat smashing into a ball, but with dreams built on anticipation. Like others who played from youth to adulthood, Slade never lost the attitude he brought to the game.

At the Ashville Athletic Field as the Champs' most experienced player, he increased his desire to excel as a long-ball hitting third baseman.

"Haven't lost a thing from your swing," Red Morrison chirped as Slade slammed pitches either over the 330-foot sign in left field or deep into center field where a sign indicated 425 feet.

"We'll need a lot of that this year," said Morrison, referring to a roster depleted since the '53 season. In addition to losing Randy Wilson, the one-season, center fielder who completed his college career at St. John's in northern Indiana and then signed with the Cleveland Indians, the Champs failed to find suitable replacements at shortstop and left field. Gone due to injuries suffered when they collided trying to catch a fly ball in the '53 title game were shortstop Sandy Anderson (shoulder) and left fielder Tom Bauer (knee).

Johnny Champion and Morrison attempted to fill the voids with new players, but some of the candidates displayed more enthusiasm than ability.

"If we could get some of these high school wonders before they go into college or pro ball, we'd be okay," Champion told Slade. "High school teams all over the area are loaded, and I wasn't surprised to read that Ted Tedesco and Rick Wagner will pitch against one another this weekend when the Big Ten Conference season opens."

Both Ashville products, right-hander Tedesco at the University of Illinois, and left-hander Wagner at Northwestern U. were No. 1 at their respective schools after storied careers on the prep and American Legion levels. At Illinois, Tedesco joined catcher Wayne Lanter (Freeburg) and outfielder Dick Pawlow (East St. Louis).

At the University of Missouri, infielders Gary Starr from Ashville High and Sonny Siebert from Bayless, Missouri, were expected to lead the Tigers.

For the Champs, the nucleus consisted of long-time starting pitcher Bob Range, catcher Vernon Koester, first baseman Ted Hill, second baseman Mark Anderson, and outfielder-pitcher Ray Smith. Others at practice caused Slade to examine Morrison's clipboard for first and last names. As a result, after removing the black spikes his sons had shined, Slade urged Champion and Morrison to meet him at the Foul Ball.

At the tavern, any intent at roster evaluation yielded to proprietor Dutch Schmidt and his observations and stories related to the new Greater County League.

"Muellers practiced yesterday," said Schmidt of the team that would share the Athletic Field with the Champs.

"They have Les Mueller, and Smokey Bruss," Schmidt said of the 28-year-old former Cleveland minor league center fielder. A .300 hitter as an 18-year-old rookie for Iola, Kansas, of the KOM League in 1948, Bruss had starred at Ashville High. In 1951, his final year as a pro, he was drafted into the Army and became a paratrooper.

"He's a tough, left-handed hitter, and should pepper that right-field screen," Schmidt said.

An easy target for the Champs' Wilson in '53, the right-field screen held a 305-foot sign and stood about 25 feet from the edge of the Richland Creek, which wound behind and past the Athletic Field.

Neither Bruss nor the screen was the main topic for Schmidt, who warned the Champs about Mascoutah in the St. Clair Division.

"They've got the toughest pitcher in the league, and some of the Muellers said they heard he's throwing harder than ever," Schmidt said of Terry Plab, who reached all-star status within two years of a tragic injury in 1953.

After placing a beer in front of Slade and bottles of Coca-Cola on the same table for Morrison and Champion, Schmidt reached in his apron pocket and produced a tattered newspaper article.

"I kept this in a scrapbook," Schmidt said. "I always think of it whenever I hear anything about Terry, or when I read about a pro ball player whining about an injury."

Headlined "Local Athlete Injured in Farm Accident," the 1953 *Mascoutah Herald* story explained how the 18-year-old Plab was nearly killed when his right leg became entangled in a hay bailer on a farm near Mascoutah.

According to the article, "After a Friday tryout with the St. Louis Cardinals at Sportsman's Park where Dick Schofield also excelled, right-hander Plab was offered a Class AAA contract that he was expected to sign two days later."

"On the Saturday after his tryout though, when he kicked at the twine used to tie the bales, rollers caught his shoestring and pulled him into the machine. Able to keep his body from being sucked inside by clinging to a platform railing, he screamed loudly enough for other workers to shut the machine off, but not before his right leg was mangled.

"It took the fire department from O'Fallon 3 1/2 hours to cut him loose. After he was taken to the hospital in Ashville, doctors saved his leg, but he was there for six months and had seven operations."

"I don't want to be rude," Morrison told Schmidt, "but we've all heard about how he wraps his leg in foam rubber and bandages before a game."

"What's helping him throw harder?" Morrison asked.

"Yesterday, those guys said there's a rumor about how he gives himself shots to kill the pain," Schmidt said.

"He owns a thoroughbred stud farm and should know how to give shots," Morrison said, "but I've heard he's so sore after a Sunday game he can hardly move for two days."

While ignoring his handicap, Plab averaged nearly a strikeout per inning and represented players with an intense passion for baseball.

"No doubt about his courage," Champion said, "but Mascoutah is like any other team in need of more than one player to win in this league."

As Schmidt attended to other customers, Slade again read the names on Morrison's clipboard and shunned dwelling on his role as the leader of the Champs or on Plab's failure to sign with the Cardinals.

Chapter 15

R egarding headlines and stories, Slade had become accustomed to seeing his name in the *Ashville News*, which thrived on balancing local and professional sports.

On the Saturday prior to Mother's Day, May 11, 1958, for instance, the *News* devoted considerable space to the Greater County League. Because the *News* did not publish on Sundays, sports editor Walter Irish, with the help of recently hired writer Joe Thompson, seized the opportunity to provide more local information than pro-related stories.

For Irish, writing the headline, "Slade Has High Hopes for Champs" was easy. The scribe had written about the athlete for nearly 20 years, and Slade had established himself as the team's most consistent hitter through championship seasons (1951 and '53) and thereafter.

On this occasion though, the Mueller Furniture team, as a second Ashville entry, justifiably earned a headline reading: "Muellers Offer Divisional Challenge."

To stir optimism for their respective St. Clair Division teams, Irish used quotes from Slade and Les Mueller related to the Champs greeting Mascoutah, and the Muellers playing at St. Libory as part of the league's 2 p.m., nine-inning, Sunday openers.

After noting outstanding players with defending St. Clair League champion Freeburg, Irish devoted special attention to '57 Monroe County League champ Waterloo and its distinguished pitching staff.

"No need to pray for Waterloo," Irish stressed. "They should have an edge with the arms of their pitching priests, right-hander Donald Eichenseer and left-hander Ed Hustedde."

Teammates at Waterloo when they were seminary students, the young Catholic priests benefited from being assigned to churches in southwestern Illinois.

In addition to the Greater County story, the *News* reported on high school events, Ashville Junior College and McKendree College games, men's and women's fast pitch softball, American Legion and youth baseball tryouts, bowling, hunting and fishing, and pigeon racing.

While Thompson's byline led readers to highlights from the Belle-Clair Speedway where stock cars and midget autos were geared for spring and summer racing, Irish used his "Brew" to express discontent with Major League baseball.

Beneath the headline "Major Leagues Have Gone to the Dogs" he wrote, "There's no reason to lock players into an organization when they are in their 20s and in the prime of their career."

"What better example than in the new Greater County League where Freeburg boasts the presence of second baseman Kent Pflasterer, who should have reached the big leagues.

"In 1953, he was 24 years old and led Brooklyn's Pueblo, Colorado, Class AA team and the Western League with a .359 batting average. In 140 games, he had 190 hits, but remained in Double A the rest of his career. He wasn't about to get a chance to advance to the major leagues where Jackie Robinson was among the second basemen ahead of him.

"He's like Ashville's Joe Schmidt, whose .441 batting average in 1939 was one of the best ever in pro baseball. *The Sporting News* compared him to Joe Medwick, the Cardinals' 1937 Triple Crown winner. But the best offer Joe got was being asked to a Class AAA spring training where he never heard a word from St. Louis general manager Branch Rickey."

By examining current Ashville minor leaguers, Irish reported on infielders Barney Elser at Colorado Springs in Class A and Alan Grandcolas at Rochester, New York, in Triple A.

"For several years, they both were .300 hitters stuck behind St. Louis fixtures like Eddie Kasko, Don Blasingame, and Dick Schofield," Irish stressed.

"Barney is 28 years old and lucky to be in the Chicago White Sox system. Grandcolas is 25 and in his sixth season with the Cardinals. Now, they're trying to make Al a catcher, but they also intend to sign Ashville catcher Bill Morton. If the Cardinals sign Bill, they have indicated he will be assigned to Albany, Georgia, in Class D with another rookie, Mike Shannon, an outfielder from St. Louis.

"If it's a big deal to say you were a big leaguer - even if ever so briefly, consider Roy Hawes of Shiloh. As a 24-year-old first baseman, he was called up to the Washington Senators for the last eight games of the 1951 season. He got a pinch-hit single in his first game on September 23 at Philadelphia. Then he went 0-for-1 in another contest, and then 0-for-4 in the final game of the season to finish 1-for-6.

"How many players would have Hawes' humility? When asked about his single off Bob Hooper, the Athletics' right-handed knuckleballer, Roy claimed he was more thrilled with being called to the majors, saying, 'I made quite a jump from Class D in one year. God moves in mysterious ways.'"

Irish concluded: "Since the Senators already had left-handed hitting all-star Mickey Vernon, they weren't about to make room for Roy. He spent the next four years with Chattanooga, Tennessee, in the Class AA Southern League. This season, he's with Milwaukee, his fourth organization on the Triple A level."

According to Irish, one of the briefest careers in Major League history belonged to Hank Schmulbach of East St. Louis, who appeared in just one game as a pinch runner.

"An outstanding second baseman at East St. Louis Senior High and at Washington U., Hank was 18 years old when he signed with the St. Louis Browns in late-September of 1943," Irish wrote.

"Immediately placed on the Browns' roster, he joined the team in Philadelphia on September 27 where he pinch ran in the ninth inning of the second game of a doubleheader. After replacing catcher Frankie

Hayes, who had walked and advanced to second base, Hank scored the sixth run in a 7-6 victory."

Irish noted how Schmulbach left baseball to serve in the U.S. Army Air Corps and returned to the Browns in 1946 for three minor league seasons, including two at Hannibal, Missouri. Among his '47 teammates was Roy Sievers, who became the American League Rookie of the Year in '49 with the Browns.

Interviewed by Irish, Hank's brother Ed, a batboy at Class C Hannibal, said, "Hank enjoyed making it to the major leagues, but he was never bitter."

In 1952, Alfred "Boots" Budde, a left-hander from Ashville, won nine games and set a Hannibal record with a 2.79 earned run average.

Irish also cited Ashville native Bud Zipfel, an 18-year-old rookie in the New York Yankees' chain. In 1957, he hit .267 with 13 home runs and 19 doubles for Greenville, Texas, in the Class D Sooner State League.

"He had 116 hits in 116 games, and currently is assigned to Auburn, New York, in the New York-Penn League, but that's another season in Class D," Irish complained. "My bet is only a trade will allow him to reach the big leagues because the Yankees have Moose Skowron, age 27, at first base. In the outfield, Hank Bauer is old at 35, but they also have Mickey Mantle, 26, and St. Louis native Norm Siebern, 24."

The word 'trade' allowed Irish to compliment the Cardinals for replacing GM Frank Lane with St. Louis native Vaughn "Bing" Devine. "When Lane talked about trading Stan Musial, he was dumber than a dog - even my pet dog Tootsie," Irish wrote.

The column appeared next to an Irish bylined story about the Cardinals (5-14) and Chicago Cubs (13-10) in a doubleheader in St. Louis where the McDaniel brothers - bonus baby Von and veteran Lindy would start for the Redbirds. Also an official scorer for the Cardinals, Irish heard from front-office types about the arm woes of 19-year-old Von, but preferred promoting the Cards-Cubs rivalry that would be among several Mother's Day highlights.

Chapter 16

On the Monday after Mother's Day, sportswriter Joe Thompson displayed his literary talents although some *Ashville News* readers may have preferred more baseball facts than exaggeration. Responsible for compiling a story on the Greater County League, he gave an account of the Ashville Champs vs. Mascoutah game at the Athletic Field, and did his best to report other results.

Initially, he was factual, giving notoriety to Terry Plab, who gained a 4-2 victory over the Champs by striking out 16 batters in nine innings, allowing six hits, and overcoming three infield errors. Within three paragraphs though, the former writer for the *Scott Air Force Base News*, offered allusions only music and/or movie fans might understand.

"Plab threw great balls of fire at the Champs," wrote Thompson with an obvious reference to the 1958 hit song, "Great Balls of Fire," by Jerry Lee Lewis. According to Thompson, "the only defiant one (used thanks to the movie "The Defiant Ones" starring Tony Curtis and Sidney Poitier), was Frank Slade, who was no palooka with two singles and a double."

Even if some readers did not know a palooka was a term for a weak boxer, Thompson stayed with a boxing theme by writing: "After hitting an easy fly ball to center field in the first inning, Slade accounted for the first extra base hit in the fourth inning when he smashed a Plab offering harder than if he were Sugar Ray Robinson smacking Carmen Basilio."

From the welterweight division, Thompson bounced to the heavyweight level and noted, "In the sixth inning, Slade's sharp single popped louder than a Floyd Patterson hook. Since the hit came after a base on balls and two infield miscues, the result was two runs batted in."

The writer then credited Champs' pitcher Bob Range before explaining how a dropped fly ball in left field with the bases loaded in the eighth inning broke a 2-2 tie.

"After that, Plab put the Champs in twilight time with the final two of his sweet little sixteen," Thompson declared.

Although the Platters, who sang "Twilight Time," and Chuck Berry, writer-singer of "Sweet Little Sixteen," may never have been associated with baseball, Thompson followed with subtle incorporation of '58 movie titles in lines used to describe other games.

From notes and a box score provided by the Muellers, he forecast a long hot summer for any team taking St. Libory lightly after the Saints had edged the Ashville team, 6-4.

"Gilbert 'Skip' Mense was a cat on a hot tin roof as he overcame the hitting of Don 'Smokey' Bruss and two other former minor leaguers, outfielder Walter 'Whip' Dill (Brooklyn) and first baseman Chuck Weiss, once a leading New York Yankees' prospect," Thompson wrote.

"One of three Mense brothers in the game, Skip Mense won 11 games in 1952 for the New York Giants' Pauls Valley, Oklahoma, team in the Class D Sooner State League. But a year or so after patrolling the 38th parallel for the U.S. Army in Korea, he hurt his pitching arm in a pickup game.

"He showed no signs of weakness with his arm or bat," Thompson claimed before crediting the right-handed pitcher/batter with a decisive two-run double off Les Mueller in the seventh inning.

Other game highlights referred to 6-foot-7 Dave Luechtefeld of St. Louis University pitching for Tilden, former White Sox minor leaguer Ron Rujawitz on the mound at Millstadt, and outfielder Nelson Mathews, a senior-to-be at Columbia High School, leading Columbia with a home run into a flower garden beyond the left-field area.

"Even the daffodils, lilacs, and tulips should fear Mathews," Thompson expressed in a fashion that would bring criticism from Walter Irish.

For Irish, writing was enjoyable, but he preferred wrapping limited opinion around specifics.

In reporting on the Cardinals' 8-7 and 6-5 victories over the Cubs, for instance, he termed the sweep another Musial tale. "With five singles, the 37-year-old future Hall of Famer is two shy of the coveted 3,000 career hit mark he is sure to pass," Irish wrote.

Although Irish could not predict that the first game would be the last Major League game for Von McDaniel, the sports editor did emphasize "wildness and five walks in two innings."

Mother's Day, indeed, had been memorable for the Ashville sportswriters. By summer, the journalists destined for diversion would have more stories for readers.

Chapter 17

Players like Slade paid little attention to the umpires in the Greater County League because of the change Lee Mathews made a few years earlier in the St. Clair League. No longer was the visiting team required to bring a home plate umpire, and the home team expected to provide a base umpire.

That arrangement placed the home team's ump on the bases where he had fewer opportunities to influence the outcome of a game than if behind the plate. To most managers, coaches, and players though, the umpires were fair and not influenced by the free post-game beers they received when the teams met at taverns.

To insure parity, Mathews gave teams a list of umpires obtained from an original pool approved by the managers. The home team then would hire two umpires per game, meaning visiting teams need not be responsible for finding an ump or paying him.

Mathews also place Bill Moore in charge of distributing an umpire list prior to the season. But should controversy or protests arise, the league would take command.

In 1957, in the St. Clair League, Mathews took control of a situation at Lebanon that became an example of his authority.

Frustrated by going hitless in four at-bats, a Lebanon player took exception to a third strike called on him in the eighth inning of a game. He followed with his best contact of the day by swinging his bat into the rib cage of the plate umpire. Knocked to the ground, the ump lost control of his balloon chest protector but was able to grip his face mask and use it to ward off the batter's fists.

Because of the alertness of the opposing catcher and the Lebanon manager, the player was pulled off the ump before more punches could be landed. The game resumed but only after the player was ejected from the game and off the field site.

Informed of the incident by both managers, Mathews phoned the umpire who said he would not press charges if the player was kicked out of the league for good.

"No problem," said Mathews before assuring the ump there would be no newspaper story. "I've told the managers if they are asked anything, to say I've handled the matter."

If word of mouth fueled exaggeration, the league president thought his strategy less of a challenge to league integrity than overblown newspaper accounts. If approached by Walter Irish, for instance, Mathews knew the sports editor could keep as quiet as he and other writers were a few years previously regarding an incident in East St. Louis.

During a game at Jones Park, a brawl erupted at home plate after a catcher's hard tag of a sliding runner. As the pile of players increased, five shots were fired into the air from the gun of a deputy sheriff, who also happened to be a coach for the host team. After the shots stopped the fighting, the game continued to its conclusion.

At East St. Louis and Lebanon, the only reporters of the game were the teams' respective score keepers. They kept an account of runs, hits and errors, but not the number of shots fired or swings by a disgruntled batter.

After six weeks of the '58 Greater County League, Mathews was pleased by the absence of protests or confrontations until a June 22 game at Freeburg.

Although the home team won, its burly catcher, a former minor leaguer, took exception to the plate umpire's call of pitches. Called out on strikes early in the game, the catcher growled later after an opponent reached on ball four.

"Why was that a strike for me, but a ball for him?" he yelped.

Hearing no response, the catcher continued to bark from the Freeburg dugout, saying, "Get your head in the game," and "Where in the hell did they find you?"

Mathews added to the catcher's plight. By parking his Buick beneath a tree and at an angle near the backstop, the president could view any extracurricular activities. In addition, when the catcher approached the umpire after the game, Mathews witnessed their confrontation less than a block from the ball park where the player and umpire had parked their cars.

The catcher, after placing a bag containing his equipment and bat in the truck of his car, shouted, "You're not getting out of here that easily?"

The umpire, already changed from his game apparel and in T-shirt and slacks, calmly stood near the driver's side of his Dodge coupe and stared.

Provoked by the silence, the catcher aggressively pushed the umpire hard into the side of the coupe. Forced to respond, the umpire made a left-hand grasp of the catcher's game jersey and quickly followed with two consecutive right-hand punches to the player's nose.

Schooled in boxing in the Air Force, the umpire then knocked his bloodied adversary into the Dodge's side mirror and radio antenna. As the mirror's glass fell to the street, the catcher slid down the side of the car. He might have slumped there longer had it not been for the arrival of a black and white police car, which pulled aside the Dodge and in front of Mathews' Buick.

"Get your ass out of here," the policeman shouted at the player. "It's about time somebody took exception to your shit."

Unknown to the umpire, the policeman - actually the Freeburg Chief of Police - was the catcher's dad.

"Here's $10 bucks for your mirror and that bent antenna," the Chief told the ump who accepted the money and left in silence.

"That okay with you?" the Chief asked Mathews after their cars sat side-by-side.

"No problem," said Mathews. "I didn't recognize the umpire. If he's a replacement, I'll make sure he's never assigned to our league again."

Alone, after pulling away, Mathews recalled saying, 'no problem,' and knew he would have to suspend the catcher. He also thought of the next league meeting where he intended to inform the managers of the incident while hoping the season would not produce more surprises.

Chapter 18

Meeting at the Foul Ball in Ashville was logical for Lee Mathews and the Greater County League because of Dutch Schmidt.

On a Monday, June 30, evening when business might have been slow, Schmidt enjoyed whetting the appetites of Mathews and others with everything from cold beer to popcorn to pretzels to the largest hamburgers in southwestern Illinois.

The massive Mathews also appreciated how the Foul Ball's décor reflected Schmidt's love of baseball. Framed team photos of the St. Louis Cardinals and Browns, and individual autographed pictures dotted the walls. Among the notables were Dizzy Dean and Satchel Paige, who pitched at the Ashville Athletic Field during their barnstorming days. More recent additions included Stan Musial, Red Schoendienst, Hank Bauer, and Bob Turley.

In an area where Mathews presided, team photos of the 1951 and '53 Ashville Champs reflected league titles. Nearby was an equally large picture of Les Mueller in a Detroit Tigers' uniform.

On this occasion though, Mathews captured the attention of the other league officers and representatives of the 14-team league, including the Champs' Red Morrison, Johnny Champion, and Slade.

"This has been a good season so far," Mathews began, "but we cannot have any more bullshit like at Freeburg."

After recounting what he witnessed and emphasizing suspension for misconduct, the league president referred to the initial purpose of the meeting - selecting all-stars for the St. Clair vs. Monroe Division game slated for Thursday, July 10.

"We're taking this game to the lighted field at Scott Air Force Base," said Mathews. "It's the idea of Mayor Jerome (Ashville Mayor Jacob Jerome). He thought it would be another way to build goodwill between the base and area communities."

"Playing on that date also fits our schedule better," Mathews said. "We cannot afford to lose another Sunday as we will on July 6 due to the Valmeyer tournament."

Placing the all-star topic on hold, Mathews urged Valmeyer manager Dennis Harold to explain the tournament format since it would include four Greater County League teams.

"There will be four games on each of the first two days and then the consolation, third-place and championship games on Sunday," Harold said in matter-of-fact fashion while handing out the tourney pairings.

"I can't thank the league enough for letting us use a Sunday as part of our tournament," Harold said. "In the future, if more Greater County teams want in, I assure you, we will make room for you."

Scheduled for tourney play were Valmeyer, Waterloo, Millstadt and the Champs of the Greater County League, Alton of the Inter City League, and the St. Louis Printers, Clark Funeral Home of St. Louis, and Cape Girardeau, Missouri, all without league affiliation.

In recent years, Cape Girardeau opposed the Champs in July Fourth weekend games at the Athletic Field. In the absence of those two teams, the Muellers were slated to oppose Jasper Tile, an East St. Louis Inter City League team, as part of Homecoming Days in Ashville.

According to Harold, baseball would be a portion of the festivities at Valmeyer. In addition to a parade and fireworks on the holiday, Borsch Memorial Park would bustle each day with concession stand activity, and each night with live music and dancing beneath a pavilion.

"It's a community thing," Harold said. "I've phoned the managers of the other teams with their schedules. They also know no one should go home without a belly full of baseball and refreshments."

Harold announced pairings, starting at 9 a.m. on Friday, July 4, with Waterloo vs. Clark Funeral, followed by Millstadt vs. Alton, the Champs vs. Cape Girardeau, and Valmeyer vs. the Printers.

The energetic manager reminded the Greater County officials that the invitational, in its fifth year, would have open rosters.

"You can bring anyone you want, but you have to submit a roster of 25 players or fewer." Harold said. "Most teams stay with their normal roster, but since some of the other Greater County teams are taking the weekend off, you might want to add someone."

Since the Champs' league roster consisted of 20 players, Champion asked Morrison and Slade if they saw a need to add a player or two for the tourney.

"Our pitching is thin, and we have room on the roster, but I'm not sure if our guys would like adding an outsider," Morrison said.

"I just want to play," said Slade before being distracted by the arrival of Walter Irish.

"Let's get to the all-star selection," Irish shouted to Mathews. "I've got a deadline to meet, and I didn't come here to hear any haggling."

Spurred by the request, Mathews turned to Bill Moore and Norm Sutter to direct the selection process.

Because players were prohibited from attending the all-star voting, Slade departed for another night shift. At work, he dwelled on his .350 batting average, 12 runs batted after eight games, and all-star qualifications. He also mentally prepared for the tourney where the achievements of May and June could be surpassed or ignored in a weekend.

Chapter 19

uly brought more than heat to Ashville. For Slade, the Tuesday *Ashville News* revealed that he had been named to the St. Clair Division all-star team. For Johnny Champion, observing a red, 1949 Ford parked across the street from the Champion's meant the return of Randy Wilson.

From the desk position once held by his father, the store heir prepared to phone Slade as the sunlight reflected off the Ford's driver's side front window and stretched through the store like a silver ribbon. In line with each of Randy's steps, the light accompanied him to the entrance and then to the front counter.

How easy for Johnny to recall being stationed there when a 20-year-old Indiana college baseball player asked where he could meet the elder Champion. This time, Johnny, again wearing a long sleeve shirt as he did in 1953 to hide his handicapped left arm, rose from behind his desk and beckoned Randy to the second level.

After a hand shake and a hug reunited the close friends from the Champs' '53 season, Johnny quickly learned the reason for Randy's return.

"I've been released," Randy said. "I found out last Friday after we got back to Mobile. I was hitting .250 when they signed some players in June and were making room all the way up and down the organization."

"But that's not why I'm here," he added. "I didn't hear of your dad's death in time to come back for the funeral, and I thought since I was driving north to Indiana and St. John's, I ought to stop and pay my respects. Without your dad, I might not have signed with Cleveland or anybody."

Aware that the Mobile, Alabama, Bears were the Class AA affiliate of the Cleveland Indians, Johnny said he had followed Randy's progress in *The Sporting News*.

"Charlie Becker phoned Mobile and asked a secretary to tell me about your dad," Randy said of the Cleveland scout who had signed him. "I didn't hear anything until after we got back from a road trip."

"Don't worry," Johnny replied. "I want to hear everything about you since you left here."

After being handed a Coca-Cola, Randy recalled his senior year at St. John's and leading the Indiana Collegiate Conference with a .400 batting average and 11 home runs.

"That convinced the Indians to sign me, and as soon as school ended, I was on my way to the Jacksonville Beach Sea Birds of the Class D Florida State League," Randy said. "I had a heck of a year and respected our manager Spud Chandler. He pitched for the Yankees in the '42 and '43 World Series against the Cardinals."

"In '55, they sent me to Class C Fargo-Moorhead of the Northern League, and I hit .305 with 13 home runs. The only other left-handed batter better than me was our catcher Ken Retzer. He said he grew up in Wood River, Illinois, and played against Ashville High."

"In '56, they sent both of us to Reading, Pennsylvania, of the Class A Eastern League. Retz is still there, but I showed enough to move up to the Southern Association last season with Mobile. That's where my problems began.

"We were playing a game in Atlanta, and their big first baseman, a guy named Dick Stuart, hit a long fly ball to centerfield. I thought I had enough room to catch it because the wall was 430 feet from home plate. But unlike when I was in college and ran into the outfield fence and caught the ball, I hit the wall in Atlanta, and didn't make the catch."

Told by Becker in 1953 of Randy's sensational catch at St. John's when he suffered a gash to the right side of his face, Johnny leaned forward to hear more.

"This time I hit my right knee on the wall and had to leave the game," Randy said. "After they carried me off the field, they may as well have carried me out of the lineup. I was hitting .310 with 15 homers when I got hurt, and I didn't play the last three weeks of the season."

As Johnny observed Randy, he wondered how his visitor accepted adversity after having been compared to Mickey Mantle.

"When I got back to St. John's where I still had a job as a dorm monitor, coach (Barton) Griffin sent me to the school doctor who said I had a slightly torn cartilage," Randy said. "I didn't need surgery, but in spring training this year, I was a step slower. About the time I thought I was getting better, I twisted the knee again."

"I knew the Indians had two older outfielders in the major leagues in Larry Doby and Minnie Minoso. There also were three younger than me - Rocky Colavito, Roger Maris, and Gary Geiger, and I was in my fifth season in the minors. When my batting average dropped, my time was limited."

Informed by Johnny that Geiger lived in Murphysboro, Illinois, about an hour drive from Ashville, Randy said it was not unusual to meet other players from the St. Louis area.

"There's great baseball here," he said. "I was lucky to play for the Champs in '53, and I improved."

The reference to luck caused Johnny to talk about the Valmeyer Tournament and its open roster.

"Look, Randy, you've driven almost 500 miles today," Johnny said. "Why not stay here tonight? The room dad let you use down the hall is still there. Tomorrow, come to our practice at the Athletic Field and say hello to Red and Frank and the other guys. If you want to, you can take a little BP."

Given those options and an invite to dinner, Randy accepted a key to the back door, leading to his former bedroom. Before departing, he again perked Johnny's curiosity by referring to a non-baseball subject.

"I stopped in Macon on my way here, and saw your cousin," Randy said.

Chapter 20

Telephone calls to Slade and Red Morrison included the news of Randy Wilson, and the possibility of Randy joining the team for games in Valmeyer.

After picking Randy up at Champion's and driving to the Dutch Girl for dinner, Johnny Champion was pleased to hear that the former Indians' prospect would practice with the Champs.

"If you want to play with us again, you can, but Frank and Red need to see if the rest of the team is on board," Johnny said.

"Sounds good to me," said Randy as he followed Johnny to a booth in a corner of the restaurant where their conversation returned to the topic of Georgia Ann Champion.

"You mentioned my cousin this afternoon," Johnny said. "Did you drive from Mobile, Alabama, to Macon, Georgia, just to find out about my dad's death?"

"No, I wanted to see her again," Randy said. "While I was playing ball, I didn't have much time for women or traveling. But now that I had time, I thought I'd stop in Macon to see how she was doing. I took a chance and drove downtown to the Capitol Theater, which she had talked about when we were together in '53."

Conscious of how Georgia Ann, a beautiful, Ava Gardner look-alike, had met Randy during her summer visit to Ashville, Johnny smiled.

"Why wouldn't she appreciate meeting a blond-haired, blue-eyed guy whose smile and deep dimple make him look like a movie star?" Johnny thought while letting Randy recall Monday's events.

"When I walked into the theater, some guy on stage was reading from a script," Randy said. "At first, I couldn't see anyone else. But as I walked down the center aisle, there was enough light for me to see Georgia sitting in the front row with a clipboard on her lap."

"After the guy read something about the sound of a woman's voice being like a melody, and the touch of her hand like a symphony, I heard Georgia say, 'thanks,' and 'next, please.'

"When no one else came out on stage, I wanted to ask her if I could give it a try, but before I reached her, she already had turned and recognized me."

"She was as surprised as I was," Randy said. "She was wearing blue jeans and a white, cotton blouse. With her dark hair, she was as pretty as ever."

"It's her theater now, isn't it?" Johnny asked.

"Yes, and she's living with her parents just three blocks from the theater," Randy said. "After I said I was on my way to Ashville, she spoke about your dad's funeral. She's convinced his death affected her dad."

"Uncle Earl is 58 - five years younger than my dad," Johnny said. "Sounds like he's afraid he could suffer a heart attack."

"You're right," Randy replied, "and that's why he has changed how he interacts with Georgia."

"In '53, she said he ruled her life and pushed her toward high society. Instead, she gained a liberal arts degree from the University of Georgia, and let her fondness for movies lead her to a degree in drama and theatrical production."

Well informed of Georgia's activities, Johnny said he knew she spent five years in college due to earning a second major.

"She did some acting in school, and after she returned to Macon, she became involved in theater productions at the Capitol," Johnny said. "Television was keeping people at home, and when the Capitol began losing money on its films, uncle Earl bought the place and gave it to Georgia. Two weeks ago, she told me she intends to refurbish the theater and bring plays to downtown Macon.

"You know she's still single, don't you?" Johnny asked.

"I got that impression after we spoke at the theater, and when she invited me to her parents' place," Randy said.

"We talked a lot, and laughed about the first time we met after she got to Ashville late one night and needed a place to sleep. Your dad had given me the room near his office, but he didn't know Georgia had a key from the previous summer."

"She remembers everything from telling me how she idolized Ava Gardner and how, after awhile, I was supposed to call her Georgia instead of Ava. We also sang 'One Home Run,' the song you wrote and sang while playing your banjo at Homecoming Day at the Fairgrounds after she and I were in a skit."

During his Macon visit with Georgia and her parents, Randy said he shared stories of Edward Champion but declined an offer to stay longer.

"I wanted to knock some miles off my drive here," Randy said. "I guess it's a coincidence, but when Georgia went back home in '53, she knew I was going back to college and baseball. Now, she's devoting her attention to her theater, and that's her love."

"You're not going to tell me you didn't kiss her goodbye?" Johnny asked.

"Oh, I kissed her," said Randy, "and as I drove away, I thought about more than that."

"I thought about when I was in college and went to our spring dance with the coed who had written a letter recommending me to the Indians. With her, I never experienced anything like when I kissed Georgia. Maybe it was because we were going our separate ways—me to pro baseball and her to teaching in Ohio."

"As I drove here, I heard the song that says, 'a kiss is just a kiss,' and I thought about Georgia."

"How about wondering if we can eat this fried chicken?" asked Johnny, who refrained the remainder of the evening from giving any hint of his plans for Randy and the Champs.

Chapter 21

After getting a good night's sleep for the first time in several weeks, Randy Wilson enjoyed revisiting the Athletic Field where he would experience an amateur baseball practice for the first time in five years.

At a corner of the left-field wall, he recognized a sign proclaiming "Home of the Champs." No longer evident were the light standards that had survived the Ashville flood of 1950 and remained in place until being removed after the '53 season.

"Amazing how 12 inches of rain in eight hours did a million dollars of damage to the city," he thought while observing the creek beyond the right-field fence.

In '53, as the Champs' center fielder, he experienced a successful summer of baseball and work that eased the memory of his parents' death. They perished in a house fire shortly after he had begun his junior year at St. John's. Thanks to the recommendation of Charlie Becker and Edward Champion, Randy found employment at the sporting goods store and a place on the men's team.

Now, after being released, he had another chance to play for the Ashville team headed for the Valmeyer Tournament. Another opportunity he quickly accepted was Johnny Champion's offer to start work after the holiday weekend and remain until returning to college in early September.

At Champion's, Randy would assist Bob Freels, the company's No. 1 salesman. In 1947, Freels led the Ashville Stags to the Class D Illinois State League championship. The title was Ashville's only one during its three-year (1947-49) affiliation - first with the Browns in '47 and '48 and then with the Yankees.

A native of Mascoutah, right-handed pitcher Freels lost his first two games in '47 and then reeled off a record of 19 consecutive wins. His streak, 19-2 record, and 2.15 earned run average were among the best ever in the minor leagues. A year later, the fifth-place Stags averaged approximately 100 spectators per home game in a season when 17-year-old Bob Turley posted a 9-3 record.

For Freels, a trade to the Cleveland organization preceded a streak of 12 wins during a 17-5 campaign when he posted a 2.83 ERA for Dayton, Ohio, in the Class A Central League. In '52, he returned to the Browns and retired after hurting his pitching arm with Class AA San Antonio, Texas.

Coincidentally, as Randy approached Johnny Champion and Red Morrison near the Athletic Field's entrance, he overheard a reference to Freels.

"When Bob was here today, we spoke about the Valmeyer Tournament," Johnny told Morrison. "He insisted I give Terry Plab a call because Mascoutah isn't playing this weekend."

Anxious to get reacquainted with Slade, Randy was greeted first by news related to himself and Plab.

"You're with us the rest of the way, and Plab is here tonight and with us at Valmeyer," Morrison said.

Pleased, Randy moved to the first base dugout where he shook hands with Slade and Plab. Also a league all-star choice, Plab was the winning pitcher against the Champs in their season opener. After eight games, he compiled a 6-2 record with 90 strikeouts in 72 innings.

During the team's batting practice, Johnny Champion placed two uniforms on top of the dugout for the two new players who also had attracted attention.

In the first round of hitting, after Slade pulled Bob Range fastballs to left field, left-handed hitting Randy drilled shots into the right-field screen. Other Champs also got the feel of success batting against Range, but things changed after Plab took the mound.

Informed that he would pitch the first game at Valmeyer, Plab displayed an easy motion as he threw to Vernon Koester, the team's regular catcher. Accustomed to pivoting and pushing on a right leg wrapped from ankle to just beneath his knee, the lanky 6-foot, 170-pound right-hander caused an occasional pop in Koester's glove when batters swung and missed.

"Save some for Friday," said Morrison after noticing how Slade's hits were of less distance than previous, and how Randy stroked pitches to left field. The manager then halted batting practice in favor of infield and outfield drills. After calling the players together, he issued Valmeyer schedules and directions to Borsch Park, and reminded everyone of the weekend festivities.

By then, Plab had returned to Mascoutah where he would rub his right leg with horse liniment and massage his right arm with a similar balm. At the Foul Ball, Slade and Randy concentrated on the past, especially after the Champs' veteran insisted on hearing about the experiences of the former minor leaguer.

Chapter 22

Sitting with Randy Wilson at the Foul Ball for the first time since 1953 was ironic and informative for Slade. Five years earlier, Randy, after being hit by a pitch during an exhibition game with the Champs at the Southern Illinois Penitentiary, had cornered Slade and asked, "Do you ever get scared?"

The response of "No" was followed by Slade recalling World War II and being shot at during the battle for the Ruhr Valley in Germany. Within seconds, he had witnessed the arrival of another Army grunt in a fox hole and then the soldier's death. Warned not to peek from their position, the soldier had become an easy target.

Appreciative of the story, Randy said he used it to diminish the pressures of pro baseball. Now, prior to another night shift, Slade became a listener to specifics he only could have imagined.

"Because I did not sign until after graduating from St. John's, I missed the first eight weeks of the minor league season in 1954, and they sent me to Jacksonville, Florida," Randy said. "When I got there, they already had cut some outfielders, and I got a chance to play right away."

"In my first game, I got a double in my first at-bat and then drove in two runs with another double against Daytona Beach, which was a farm club of the Cardinals. Hitting and winning kept me in center field the rest of the season. I knew Jacksonville was in Class D and one of 163 minor league teams, but I was making $175 a month and playing.

"You might remember our manager Spud Chandler from when he pitched for the Yankees. Our leading hitter was our catcher Russ Nixon. He made it to the major leagues with Cleveland last year. He signed out of high school in Cincinnati in '53 and told me what to expect. He also was unique because our first baseman was his twin brother Roy.

"I never played on a team with twin brothers or saw twins on the same team. Having them at Jacksonville could have been an attendance gimmick, but they were good ballplayers. The last I heard, Roy was with Reading in the Eastern League."

Learning about the Nixon brothers did little for Slade. As a parent of twin boys, he was aware of the O'Brien twins - Johnny and Eddie, who played for Pittsburgh in the major leagues in 1956 and '57. As a result, Slade asked Randy about the pitching.

"We had a heck of a right-hander named Ray Konkoleski." Randy said. "He also was a rookie, but his $1,500 bonus and 22 wins made him more valuable to the Indians.

Told how the Sea Birds lived in cramped apartments near the Atlantic Ocean and received $1.75 per day for meal money when the team traveled, Slade sought a return to his subject by saying, "I meant the pitching you faced."

Without hesitating, Randy spoke of batting against numerous pitchers whose wildness was discounted by scouts seeking velocity.

"Maybe being thrown at in that prison game helped," Randy said. "I became patient and selective."

More important to Slade was Randy saying, "There wasn't anything you couldn't have handled. I don't care if it was their fastball or breaking pitches, you would have hit as well as I did."

Hitting was not the only compliment for Slade.

"You could have handled all the stuff besides the baseball," Randy said.

"What do you mean by stuff?" Slade asked.

"There's more to pro baseball than the games," Randy said. "My summer in Ashville prepared me for some of it. You remember when I turned 21, and I got an ass full of beer from the tavern stops we made during our drive home from the prison."

"I haven't done much drinking since then, but in pro ball, regardless of where I played, there were guys who thought they could drink as much as they wanted, and it wouldn't affect them. If it wasn't the booze, the 'Baseball Annies' would get 'em."

Not familiar with "Baseball Annies," Slade learned about women who try to hook up with ballplayers. He also heard about an evening after a night game when the Sea Birds were leaving for Orlando.

"The whole ball club was on the bus near the entrance to the ball park," Randy said. "Just before Spud got on the bus, I was seated in the back across from one of our infielders when I heard the damndest sound from a window on his side.

"It sounded like someone running their finger nails down a black board. In this case, it was caused by a dark haired woman trying to see inside the bus. She must have broken several nails trying to get the player's attention. Each time she'd jump to look in, he'd slouch lower into his seat, allowing her to see only the top of his Sea Bird hat.

"Then I heard Spud yell, 'Let's get out of here.' The next thing I knew we were pulling away, and she was yelling, 'You promised me you son of a bitch.'

"Her language was one thing, but I still can hear what some of the guys said when they caught a full view of her dark tan and tight blouse."

Randy also recalled another instance when the team bus broke down and the players piled into pickup trucks to complete a trip. Other highlights included his playing in Fargo-Moorhead in the Northern League in 1955 - two years after Roger Maris starred there.

"During my first bus trip from Canada to Fargo, I learned about a team tradition," Randy said.

"One of the rookies always had to sit in the front seat because the driver was a cigar smoker. And, whenever his cigar went out, he'd start dozing off at the wheel."

Startled, Slade asked, "How'd you keep from having a wreck?"

"The rookies were told to nudge the driver to keep him awake, or give him a new cigar if the one he was smoking was about to go out," Randy said.

Still curious, Slade asked, "What was the manager doing all that time?"

"He'd be asleep in the seat behind the rookie," Randy said.

With a .305 batting average and 12 home runs per season, Randy progressed. Yet, being on a higher level of competition did not guarantee improved play by his teammates or by opposing players—as Slade would learn.

Chapter 23

Before leaving for work, Slade sought more of Randy Wilson's first-person account. By sitting a comfortable distance from Dutch Schmidt and patrons playing a dice game called "Ship, Captain, and Crew," the baseball pair enjoyed solitude.

"Were there guys you played with or against who were not as good as you, but who got to higher levels of the minors or to the major leagues?" Slade asked.

"After my first year, we all knew players receiving a bonus were given more opportunities," Randy said. "If a guy was good, you'd know it, but there was no guarantee he'd move up. Who played ahead of you made a big difference. And, if a big league team sent a player to Triple A, somebody else would have to be dropped to a lower classification or released.

"When I saw Russ Nixon play, I never doubted he'd advance, but being in the right place at the right time helped. When Jim Hegan was Cleveland's regular catcher, he was 36 and a right-handed hitter. Russ was 22 and a left-handed hitter with two batting titles in his first three seasons in the minors. He's earned the chance to catch a guy like Mudcat Grant."

Mention of Jim Grant, one of Randy's teammates at Reading, Pa., of the Class A Eastern League, allowed Randy to return to the subject of the quality of play in the minor leagues.

"The pitching got better from Class D to Class A, and the hitters were more consistent because pitchers weren't as wild. But you never knew what might happen in a game," Randy said.

"We were in Syracuse one night near the end of the season in '56, and I witnessed one of the strangest plays I'd ever seen.

"It began when a left-handed batter for us hit a slow roller down the first base line. The pitcher fielded it, but instead of throwing to first base for an easy out, he threw the ball back to his catcher. Apparently, he did that because the catcher was just a few feet from our guy, who had stopped running after leaving the batter's box.

"There were a lot of nos. No outs, no one on base, and no one thinking because rather than throwing to first base for the out, the catcher chased the batter.

"When he couldn't make the tag, he threw to the first baseman. But by then, the first baseman had vacated the bag and come down the line toward home plate as if in a run-down play like you might see between the other bases. The first baseman then tossed the ball to the catcher, who finally threw to the second baseman who had moved to cover first base. He tagged the bag for the out.

"It was like 'Who's on First?' Abbott and Costello would have laughed their asses off."

As Slade shook his head in disbelief, Randy expanded on a variety of subjects - long bus rides, poorly lit ball parks, flannel uniforms handed down from the major leagues, card games and card tricks amongst the players, half-price beer nights, autograph signing, spectators razzing players, and arguments between managers and umpires.

"I also got to see a lot of tits," Randy said before quickly erasing Slade's surprised look with an explanation of witnessing numerous cow-milking contests at home plate.

"The promotions never ended," Randy continued.

"I was in three weddings at home plate for a bride in her gown and the groom in his baseball uniform, but when a team wanted to make money, nothing attracted fans like Jackie Price and Max Patkin."

As a reader of *The Sporting News*, Slade knew of Price's antics. Besides hitting batting practice pitches while hanging upside down, he would shoot baseballs out of an air gun and then jump into a jeep and speed into the outfield to catch the balls, or place three baseballs in one hand and accurately throw them to three different catchers.

Patkin was known more for his facial contortions and the baggy uniform he wore while mimicking players or umpires. Hired often by Cleveland owner Bill Veeck to entertain as a first base coach, Patkin began barnstorming in 1949 after Veeck sold the Indians.

"Veeck was the reason the Indians held spring training in Arizona," Randy said. "They've been in Tucson since 1947, and I was there in '57 after having my best year in the minors at Reading. I hit over .300 again, and finished with 18 home runs and 95 runs batted in."

"In Tucson, I was excited but realistic. Colavito, Maris, and old Yankee Gene Woodling were among the outfielders ahead of me. Russ Nixon was there and introduced me to Herb Score, who less than two months later he was hit in the face by a line drive off the bat of the Yankees' Gil McDougald.

"I also got to meet Hoyt Wilhelm. He told me he didn't start throwing his knuckleball until he was in high school in North Carolina. He said he read about Dutch Leonard and started to experiment with the pitch. That's when I told him about playing in the Southern Illinois Penitentiary where the athletic director was Roger Wolff. According to Edward Champion, Wolff was part of the only four-man, knuckleball pitching rotation in Major League history."

Slade then interrupted and spoke of Wolff, Dutch Leonard, and Mickey Haefner from Illinois, and Johnny Niggeling from Iowa.

"Wilhelm pitched for the Giants in the '54 World Series against Cleveland," said Slade before allowing Randy to continue.

"In spring training, I was one of three invitees from Class A," Randy said. "I got into a few games, got a couple of singles, and was used mostly as a defensive replacement or pinch runner. Then, Kerby Farrell, our manager, called me in one day and said I was being sent to Class AA and Mobile. When I consider how I struggled this season and then the injury, I'm sure I won't be remembered in Mobile like Hank Aaron and Satchel Paige."

In addition to saying he knew Aaron and Paige were born in Mobile, Alabama, Slade admitted having spoken with Johnny about Randy's crash into an outfield wall and injured knee.

"Are you going to have surgery on your knee?" Slade asked.

"At this point, I'm not sure," Randy said. "I knew a basketball player at St. John's who tore a cartilage and had to have it cut on. The scar looked like a line on a map from Indiana to Ashville."

"Every time I played, there were scouts from other organizations watching. But I haven't heard anything from anybody. I intend to visit Charlie Becker in Indianapolis to thank him for signing me. If I leave pro ball, I always can put my physical education degree to work."

Grateful for the chance to speak with Randy, Slade thanked him for coming back to Ashville and playing with the Champs one more time.

"Let's have some fun at Valmeyer," said Slade before asking one final question. "Are you bitter about your minor league experience?"

"How can I be?" Randy answered. "According to *The Sporting News,* in 1954 there were over 3,500 minor league players trying to make one of the 16 Major League teams. I heard players complain about not getting a fair shot, but after I got to Fargo-Moorhead in '55, I thought about Joe Bauman. He hit 72 home runs in 1954 at Roswell, New Mexico, in his sixth year in Class C. He never reached the big leagues and was out of pro ball after 1956.

"I was lucky," said Randy as he stood to say goodbye and then smiled. "Was that your knee cracking or mine?" he asked.

Chapter 24

While speaking with Slade, Randy Wilson dominated the dialogue. However, the next morning, in conversation with Johnny Champion, Randy entered a reversed role. Seeking details of Johnny's personal life since the two met in '53, he took advantage of the time while awaiting the arrival of Bob Freels.

"What did you do after I left for St. John's?" Randy asked.

"Well, you knew Dad expected me to take over the business," Johnny said. "As soon as I got out of high school, he wanted me to get a college degree."

"Fortunately, I was able to attend McKendree College in Lebanon. It's only a half-hour drive to campus, and dad liked that because it didn't take me far from him."

Reminded of how Johnny seemed to survive the demands of Edward Champion, Randy asked about Johnny's college experience.

"Did you just get a degree to please him?" Randy asked.

"I'm sure he was proud of my business degree, but at McKendree I also selected a minor in music," Johnny said.

"That's an unusual combination," Randy said, "but not surprising after watching you play the banjo and sing at the Fairgrounds."

Not wanting to dwell on Johnny's handicap, the result of a tree limb breaking loose and crushing his left arm after he had fallen from a tree, Randy continued.

"Were you able to put the business degree to use?" he asked.

"Yes, and dad was pleased when I suggested creating a sales staff and offering an expanded product line to more than just the schools in the immediate Ashville area," Johnny said.

"To be honest, the music classes were more difficult at times. I could sing and play the banjo or the guitar, but in one class, we had to write original lyrics. I only got a 'C.'"

After having witnessed Johnny's rendition of "One Home Run," at Homecoming Day in '53, Randy was amazed.

"Why didn't you submit 'One Home Run?' he asked.

"I thought I'd try something else, but our instructor—a woman, said it was too trite," explained Johnny, whose grade stirred doubt in Randy.

"Let me hear it," said Randy with a request that led to Johnny reciting, rather than singing what he called 'Our National Pastime.'"

Leaning back in his office chair, Johnny closed his eyes, and said:

"It's our national pastime
this game of glad times
with its hits, runs,
cheers, and roars.

"It's our favorite game
one we all have played
or watched while
wanting more.

"Let's salute it now
this game of wow
that causes young
and old to adore.

"Here's to our pastime
this game of glad times
let's cheer it
more and more."

"Sounds better than a 'C' to me," Randy said. "Didn't she like baseball?"

"I don't know," Johnny said. "When I submitted 'One Home Run,' she was more interested in my playing the banjo than my singing."

"My reason for staying with a baseball topic is no different than why I'm continuing to support the Champs," Johnny said.

"I never objected to my dad forcing me to follow the game even though I couldn't play after I was hurt. I love to watch baseball because the games are never the same. It's kind of like life. No two days are the same, and you never know what's in store for you."

Johnny also explained how his musical ability allowed him to join a campus chorus and a theatrical group.

"It wasn't like I was on the Muny stage in St. Louis," Johnny said.

Curiosity then caused Randy to ask, "Did you find a girl friend at McKendree?"

"I met some wonderful people and had a couple of dates, but I haven't been seriously involved with anyone," Johnny said. "Since dad is gone, I'm concentrating on the business."

"Well, I had to ask," Randy replied. "Besides that, you've always had a steady job, and you're driving your dad's fancy Lincoln Capri. And, don't forget, you wanted to know if I kissed Georgia."

"And, I'm as handsome as you," said Johnny, smiling as he pointed to the front door and the presence of Freels.

Walking with briefcase in hand, the former minor leaguer turned salesman looked toward the loft and loudly proclaimed: "Get ready for Valmeyer; Plab's rarin' to go."

Chapter 25

I f Bob Freels bragged about having a hand in the Champs' obtaining Terry Plab for the Valmeyer Tournament, his words did not carry the impact of Walter Irish and Joe Thompson in the Thursday afternoon edition of the *Ashville News*.

In a story headlined "Dandy Randy Returns" Irish dwelled on the Valmeyer tourney where he forecast the Champs "could be as hot as a firecracker during the holiday."

"Besides adding former minor league outfielder Randy Wilson to the roster, they borrowed Mascoutah's Terry Plab," Irish wrote.

After recalling the Champs' 1953 season and Wilson's contributions, Irish indicated how all-star pitcher Plab was ideal for the July Fourth weekend event.

According to Irish, "Injuries may have affected the baseball careers of Wilson and Plab, but they and Frank Slade, who is among the current Greater County League leading hitters, are bound to contribute."

In a separate story headlined "Muellers Ready for Weekend," Thompson explained how the other Ashville team would take the place of the Champs in games against Jasper Tile of East St. Louis.

"Jasper Tile is leading the Inter City League and will be an able replacement for Cape Girardeau, which again will test the Champs, but this time in Valmeyer," Thompson predicted.

"Adding to the Homecoming Days (expanded from a one-day celebration in '53) will be the homecoming of pitcher Ted Tedesco for the Muellers. He ranked among the Big Ten Conference pitching leaders at the University of Illinois, and is visiting during a few days off from the Basin Collegiate League in South Dakota. Since his dad Sam and Les Mueller are familiar with each other from the furniture business, it's a solid fit.

"With Mueller drawing on his Major League experience, and Tedesco throwing a baffling curveball, the Muellers should be a challenge for Jasper Tile in their Friday-Saturday series at the Athletic Field. The Inter City team, though, has a solid pitching staff with former Pittsburgh minor league right-hander Bill Hartoin, and left-hander Kent Weisenstein, a student at the University of Missouri-Rolla."

Thompson concluded by referring to the events at the Fairgrounds.

"Any person with an accurate throwing arm should try hitting the metal target attached to the seat of Dutch Schmidt. He's a civic-minded tavern proprietor willing to be dunked when proceeds go to the Ashville Little League."

Although invited to be one of the announcers of games at Valmeyer, Irish used his "Irish Brew" to promote the baseball and Homecoming Days at Ashville.

"The presence of Les Mueller, the pride of Ashville, at the games and at the Fairgrounds, where he has agreed to sign autographs for charity, should be incentive for any baseball fan to attend," Irish stressed.

"How often do you get to meet someone who set a Major League pitching record and also hurled for a World Series championship team?" Irish asked before mentioning how fans might enjoy touching Mueller's World Series ring or listening to a story or two.

"Maybe they will hear something like this," wrote Irish as an introduction to Mueller telling of an incident that tested his calm demeanor before he reached the big leagues in 1941.

"It was my first spring training with Detroit in Lakeland, Florida," Mueller said. "I won 18 games the year before at Beaumont in the Texas League, and the Tigers were taking a good look at me."

"One day I was in the bullpen, and one of the coaches wanted to see how I gripped my fastball. When I showed him, he said I shouldn't have tucked the thumb of my throwing hand under the ball the way I did, and that I needed to change that.

"I said I'd give it a try, and after I threw a couple of pitches, he walked away. Later, he said he was watching from a distance and could tell I was throwing a better fastball.

"I thanked him, but all I did was grip the ball the way I always did. I wasn't about to tell him his idea wouldn't help me."

Irish closed by noting how time had passed since Mueller was a 22-year-old rookie.

"He's nearing age 40 and is a far cry from when he shut out the New York Yankees on two hits and faced just 28 batters in the process," Irish emphasized. "Regardless, he remains as humble as when he struck out 30 batters in a 12-inning high school game and became Ashville's hottest pro baseball prospect."

Adept at expressing an opinion or telling a story, Irish had no idea of the column-worthy items awaiting him in Valmeyer.

Chapter 26

By attending the Valmeyer Tournament and reporting on it in 1957, Walter Irish became familiar with the village, its history, and love of baseball. In addition to functioning as a sports editor, he participated as a game announcer from a perch atop the ground level, concrete, first-base dugout and endeared himself enough with tourney organizers to be invited back.

To assist with the advance publicity of the '58 tourney, he had received a book of facts on Valmeyer from longtime resident and historian Dennis Knobloch, who was preparing for the village's 50th anniversary in 1959.

As Irish guided his 1952 Chevrolet two-door Bel Air past Waterloo and onto Route 156 toward Valmeyer, he outlined plans for Joe Thompson.

"I'm staying for all four games today," Irish said. "You can take my car back to Ashville after the morning games so you can cover the Muellers. I'll ride with Red and Frank after the last game."

"We didn't publish today, but I want to load the Saturday edition with local baseball. The Cardinals are in Los Angeles. They played a doubleheader yesterday, and are not playing today. That will give us extra space. Keep your stories tight and knock off the foolish description. Since we don't publish on Sunday, our Monday stories will have to be terse because they will include six games prior to Sunday. The Muellers are playing Jasper Tile on Friday and Saturday, and Valmeyer has four games on Saturday."

Pointing to a sign indicating "Valmeyer 7 miles," Irish stressed how he valued the young reporter's presence.

"I'm in my mid-60s and alone since my wife ran off several years ago," Irish said. "Sports are my life. When it comes to covering baseball, I like this as much as when I'm in the press box at Cardinals games."

"You're 26 years old, single and starting out after reporting for the *Air Force News*. Enjoy this. Who knows what the future holds?"

Appreciative of the advice, the slim, 6-foot-2 Thompson stretched his legs on the floorboard of the passenger side and observed the sports editor. In a matter of months, Thompson understood why the bespectacled Irish was easily identified throughout the southwestern Illinois area. Despite a portly waistline and inability to keep ketchup or mustard from staining the white shirts he wore year round, the editor-columnist maintained a well-trimmed, black-pencil mustache and neatly groomed gray hair.

"You've been kind to me from the time you hired me, and today is just another example," Thompson said. "I'm just a kid from Idaho who landed at Scott Air Force Base and thought this would be a good place to start rather than going back home to pick potatoes."

After the Chevy passed the Monroe County Fairgrounds and then fields of corn and beans, Irish spoke of the caliber of folks he'd meet at Valmeyer.

"They work hard, play hard, and respect anyone who respects them," said Irish while handing the youthful looking sportswriter stapled pages penned by Knobloch.

"Read it, and you'll appreciate how three floods in the 40s could not stop them from pulling together as a community," Irish said.

As they passed signs reading "Deer Hill Road," and "Salt Lick Point," Thompson read aloud: "According to local lore, the village of Valmeyer, Illinois, got its name through the combination of Valley and Meyer. Valmeyer may have been associated with the St. Louis Valley Railroad or the Mississippi Valley. The village lies on the eastern edge of a broad flood plain called the American Bottom. The Bottom is bounded by a line of limestone bluffs on the east and by the Mississippi River to the west.

"Meyer was the name of the family of Frederick and Elizabeth Meyer. They built a large, two-story farm house, the first house on the original site of Valmeyer. In 1906, Meyer City was changed to Valmeyer, and on December 4, 1909, seven years after the first lot was sold in the town, the Village of Valmeyer was officially chartered with the State of Illinois.

"Rich in terms of fertile soil and agricultural yields, Valmeyer, by its location, also was prone to flooding. The construction of a government levee, completed in 1947 by the U.S. Corps of Engineers, was met with cheers and expected to end the destruction caused by the Mississippi River."

The word flooding caused Irish to say, "Doesn't matter if it's a river in Valmeyer or a creek in Ashville, flood waters make their own boundaries."

Thompson then referred to Knobloch indicating how the village expanded after the construction of a railroad line extending from St. Louis to Cairo, Illinois, and a side track linking Valmeyer and its limestone bluffs to a quarry in Columbia, Illinois.

By coincidence, as they passed a highway caution sign reading "Falling Rock," Irish took his right hand off the steering wheel and pointed down as the car made a steady descent toward Borsch Park.

"I can smell the bratwurst, pork cutlets, and barbeque pork steaks," he joked before telling Thompson of the food and drink available at the concession stands whose proceeds would go to community projects.

"You'll have fun here," Irish said. "Baseball games, a parade, fireworks at dusk, and music and dancing. That's how Valmeyer celebrates the Fourth."

"And, whatever you do, remember you are ineligible to answer any of the trivia questions for prizes," Irish said.

"For instance, if I ask, 'What was the first business in Valmeyer?' you say nothing about a tavern. And, if I ask, 'what's a dinky?' you say nothing about the small steam locomotive and passenger car that ran daily through Valmeyer either going to Chester or back to St. Louis."

"Don't worry, I won't say anything" Thompson said. "But it's nice to know what a dinky is."

Chapter 27

U nable to appease his appetite, Walter Irish directed his senses elsewhere as he and Joe Thompson drove past the St. John's Cemetery and turned right onto Quarry Road toward a parking lot behind the Borsch Park grandstand.

"That's Mel" Irish said after hearing the voice of Mel Lynn, the Valmeyer Tournament announcer.

"We've got a beautiful day, and four baseball games, but we can't get started until we have lineups and rosters," said Lynn from atop the first-base dugout where he sat on a picnic bench beneath a huge umbrella.

"Sounds like he's fired up" Thompson told Irish as two, metal speakers, sitting atop each end of the shingled dugout, amplified Lynn's comments.

As Lynn referred to only a half hour remaining prior to the 9:30 a.m. first game between Waterloo and Clark Funeral Home of St. Louis, Irish removed a scorebook, clipboard, and towel from the trunk of his car.

"He's just getting started, and he'll be here every day," said Irish before giving a brief description of Lynn.

"He's originally from Ashville and played first base for four years in the Cardinals' organization. After he came home, he moved to a house between Millstadt and Columbia and then played for Valmeyer for a few years. After he quit playing, he continued to support the team in any way he could."

During their walk to the dugout, Irish told of Lynn having a law degree from St. Louis University and working as a vice-president at a small college in St. Louis. While listening, Thompson stared at the ball park.

"What's a caboose doing out there?" he asked, pointing to the brightly painted red railroad car situated just outside the center field fence.

"That's a reminder of how much the railroad has meant to Valmeyer," Irish said. "One of their civic groups - the Jaycees, bought it and moved it here. I've been told if any ball player hits the caboose with a home run during the tournament, he wins a prize."

Thompson's curiosity increased when he gazed at a scoreboard in right field where a sign indicating "Alois and Twyla (Miller) Luhr Field" reflected the donations of the Luhr family and its construction company.

"It's looks as good as any big league scoreboard," Thompson said.

"They do things right here," Irish said while urging the newcomer to follow him to a ladder behind the dugout and then up rungs leading to Lynn.

Introduced to fans as "Ashville's wizards of words," Irish encouraged Thompson to enjoy the view.

"Did Abner Doubleday envision something like this when he designed a baseball field in a cow pasture in Cooperstown, New York?" Irish asked Lynn and Thompson.

According to Knobloch and other Monroe County historians, baseball in Valmeyer dated to the early 1900s when the Red Feathers opposed the nearby Foster Pond Cream Puffs. Those teams also played on what had been pasture land. By 1927, when Valmeyer High School won the Monroe County title at its Lake Street location, baseball continued to increase in popularity, and the presence of men's teams boosted interest for another diamond.

Named after Harold Borsch, a primary promoter for the construction of the new ballpark, the Valmeyer diamond was completed in the early 1950s and became a jewel in a flood plain. Located four miles east of the Mississippi River, Borsch Park sat about eight feet higher than the rest of the village. A covered grandstand with chair back seating for approximately 250 spectators, and two concession stands contributed to the baseball setting.

Natural aspects added appeal in the form of a tree-covered bluff overlooking the left-field corner and a trio of tall oak trees standing like sentries beyond the left-field fence. Between the fence and the trees, a street provided more than a parade route. Not only could visitors park their cars perpendicular to the street, they could sit in the same location and view a variety of activities throughout the day.

"How about those bleacher creatures in left field?" Lynn asked. "They look like they're ready for a parade and baseball."

By then, Waterloo had won the first game 3-1. While East Alton and Millstadt competed in the second game, a parade of a different sort dotted the Quarry Road as the Champs arrived in automotive tandem behind Red Morrison and his passenger Slade.

As the team gathered near Johnny Champion and Terry Plab, the distant sounds of a marching band gave notice of an actual parade and Valmeyer's readiness for a holiday celebration.

Chapter 28

By sitting on the third base side of the grandstand, the Champs could watch baseball or the progress of the parade as it moved from the heart of Valmeyer, around a corner filling station, and onto the street beyond left field.

With a population of 600, the village might have been host to a brief parade. On this day though, the significance of the July Fourth/Independence Day holiday attracted representatives of nearby communities eager to participate.

Led by members of the Veterans of Foreign Wars and American Legion in military dress, the parade maintained a patriotic theme enhanced by the Valmeyer High School band's rendition of "The Stars and Stripes Forever" and grade school children carrying miniature flags and red, white, and blue balloons.

To avoid the monotony of civic and youth groups filing one-by-one past onlookers, organizers placed each marching group in front of a convertible carrying a homecoming queen candidate from the Monroe County area. In addition to other high school and grade school units and cheerleaders, individuals on foot included political figures, Future Farmers of America members, Boy Scouts and Girl Scouts, women's auxiliary groups, candy-tossing clowns, and a nine-foot tall Uncle Sam on stilts. The blare of fire truck horns and the rumble of tractors eliminated any occasional silence.

After reaching the end of the road in left field, the parade wound to the right, past a pavilion and onto a parking lot off the first base side of Borsch Park. At the rear of the procession, the brass and woodwind dominated Griesedieck Marching Brigade greeted the park and ball field.

Whether playing "Beer Barrel Polka" or the "No Beer Polka," also known as "In Heaven There Is No Beer," the adult group clad in Bavarian lederhosen, white shirts, and suspenders created toe-tapping tones. As they gathered for a brief concert on a road behind the grandstand, the Alton-Millstadt game stole attention.

Trailing 4-3 in the bottom of the ninth inning, Alton had the bases loaded with no outs, meaning the winning run was at second base. With its No. 4 batter at the plate, the Inter City team appeared on the verge of advancing to a semifinal game against Waterloo. The odds increased when the cleanup hitter sent a shot down the first base line.

After the crack of the bat, the robust Alton manager positioned in the third base coaching box, assumed the best. Waving his right arm in a circular motion, he encouraged his runners to advance, without anticipating the unexpected.

Because the Millstadt first baseman was left-handed and had been playing close to the foul line, his right foot was planted in the path of the line drive. When the ball struck him just above his ankle, it ricocheted into the air toward the second baseman, who caught the ball for the first out. After alertly tagging second base for the second out, he threw to the first baseman for a tag of that base to complete a triple play and end the game.

"That's the kind of exciting action you can see at Valmeyer!" said Lynn before lowering his tone and explaining that Alton had moved into a Saturday morning consolation game against Clark Funeral, and that Millstadt had advanced to a game against Waterloo.

Stunned by the reality of the base umpire's final out call, the Alton manager, known as "Big Cat," stood with head bowed and hands on knees. As the Champs quietly moved toward the third base dugout, Lynn spoke of the odds against a triple play "being at least ten thousand to one." His estimate only added to the demise of a Cat destined to drown his sorrows.

For the Champs, optimism prevailed in the form of Terry Plab, but mound security did not keep Red Morrison from seeking more offense. Unlike in 1953 when Randy Wilson batted third and Slade fourth, the manager switched them in the batting order and gave an explanation.

"Frank, you've been hot, and you'll get better pitches to hit if you're in front of Randy." Morrison said. "Besides that, Randy, everybody knows you are home from pro ball, and if Cape Girardeau remembers you from '53, they're not about to pitch around Frank."

Because both players agreed, Morrison avoided having to offer rationale related to Randy's injured right knee. Fortunately, Plab became the focal point with 13 strikeouts in a brisk, 4-1, four-hit victory. In the process, Slade ripped two doubles for three runs batted in, and Wilson singled twice and had one RBI.

Defensively, Randy was flawless in center field where his concentration was put to a test. In the sixth inning, after catching a fly ball that had disappeared momentarily in a cloud of smoke from a barbecue stand, he increased his intensity after hearing Lynn say, "That's why I love this tournament."

Unaware that his microphone was "live," Lynn encouraged Irish to look toward left field. That suggestion allowed Irish, grandstand fans, and bleacher creatures to observe the former parade route where a shapely young blonde walked and waved. Dressed in Daisy Mae style, featuring a red and white, polka-dot blouse knotted just above her midriff, Capri pants, and high heels, she was a replica of the pursuer of Li'l Abner in the Dogpatch comic strip.

"You didn't even look at her," one of the Champs said to Randy after he had chased down a deep fly ball to end the inning.

"Blame it on Hardrock Simpson," said Randy in reference to once playing in a minor league game when a guy named Paul 'Hardrock' Simpson ran around the interior of the ballpark during the entire game as part of a promotion.

"He was famous for running across the country from Los Angeles to New York," Randy said. "Somebody said he once beat a horse in a race. I didn't care as long as I didn't have to worry about colliding with him."

Assured of a semifinal game, the Champs did not have to wait long to identify their opponent. As the sun set, Valmeyer completed an 8-1 rout of the St. Louis Printers, allowing Lynn to close with reminders to the growing number of spectators.

"Fireworks in about an hour, and music under the pavilion tonight," he said. "Happy Birthday America!" he added, knowing from experience how memorable events could evolve during a hot, summer holiday.

Chapter 29

I f inviting Walter Irish to assist as an announcer at Valmeyer meant increased publicity, the sports editor responded in excellent fashion with a Saturday *Ashville News* sports page dominated by the Champs, other tourney results, and emphasis on the semifinal pairings.

In the absence of wire service reports about the idle St. Louis Cardinals, Irish had room for a headline reading "Plab, Slade Slay Cape" on the left side of the page balanced by "Muellers Defeat Jasper Tile" on the right. Besides dwelling on the Champs' first appearance in the tourney and task of opposing the host Lakers, he used his column for details of the triple play that slew Alton.

"A triple play is rarity in itself, but how often has one ended a game?" he asked.

Joe Thompson emphasized pitching in the Muellers' 4-2 triumph at the Athletic Field where Ted Tedesco out dueled another Ashville native, Jasper Tile pitcher Bill Hartoin.

"Southwestern Illinois products continue to contribute to Homecoming Days," Thompson wrote before expanding on the hitting of Bob Klube of New Athens, who sparked the Muellers with a home run and a double and three runs batted in.

"He's been out of the minor leagues for six years after playing the outfield in the New York Giants and the St. Louis Browns organizations, but he's showing why he belongs in pro ball," Thompson noted.

Baseball was a fitting source for stories in Ashville or Valmeyer, but for Irish, conversation during the rain delay in the seventh inning of Saturday's first consolation game led to a story not fit for print. Chased from their dugout site by what locals called a "river rain," Irish and Melvin Lynn found refuge beneath the grandstand where they huddled with Valmeyer manager Dennis Harold.

"Look at the Cat," Lynn said. "He's got a 2-1 lead and should be happy."

"He was sitting there like that when I got here this morning," said Harold, whose wry smile drew inquisitive looks from Lynn and Irish.

"He's sleeping," Irish said of the 250-pound manager who slouched in a corner of the third base dugout with head down, hat pulled low, arms crossed, and feet extended.

"I think he slept there last night," said Harold before providing an account from an evening when, as the Valmeyer manager said, "The Cat was on the prowl."

"From what he told me and from what others said, he stayed for the two games after he lost yesterday," Harold said. "Then, after one of his players borrowed his car to drive to a motel in Waterloo where the team stayed, the Cat filled his belly with food and beer, and watched the fireworks.

"After he got tired of talking about the triple play at the beer stand, he walked over to the pavilion where he must have thought the live music and dancing would be a change of pace. Shortly after he sat on a bench there, a girl from one of the concession stands approached him. She's in her 20s and has the type of personality anybody would like."

The word "personality," caused Lynn to ask, "Did she look like Daisy Mae?"

"No, she was wearing one of those Bavarian outfits like the marching brigade," Harold said. "But she filled it well enough to catch the Cat's eye. They were seen dancing, but then they disappeared and must have gone for a ride in her car.

"Everybody in Valmeyer knows she bought a bright red car because she's a Cardinal fan. Regardless, I'm sure the Cat had other things on his mind than taking a ride after midnight or talking about the Cardinals."

To the dismay of Lynn and Irish, Harold spoke of the options of the 1958, two-door Nash Rambler American. Among its perks were reclining front seats, which advertisers claimed, "Could adjust to five comfortable positions."

As the rain increased, the manager put on a pair of boots and continued: "The Cat didn't say anything else about what happened after she drove them on the levee road, but my cousin Ron is one of our two village cops, and he filled me in."

"Apparently, after she parked the car, she must have explained some of the benefits of her Nash because when Ron got there, the front seats were down."

Confused, Irish asked: "Why was your cousin there?"

"Well, first you need to hear about another feature of her Nash," Harold said. "For a few extra bucks, she had an automatic dome light installed. It turns on whenever a door is opened.

"The problem for her and the Cat was his big body, so they opened a door for more room. But they couldn't relax because of the dome light.

"Ron said what attracted him while he was patrolling was a light that kept flashing on an off. At first, he said he wondered if it was from Valmeyer's first UFO. Then he thought it must have been some kind of warning light.

"My guess is since the passenger side door was the one they opened, the Cat must have asked her to kick off her sandals and use one of her toes to push in the button in the door frame to keep the light off.

"Because Ron drove toward them without using his headlights, they didn't know he parked about 60 feet behind them. He said when he approached the car, he could hear her singing "Magic Moments," but the song ended after he tapped the trunk of the car with his flashlight."

Before Harold could continue, Irish asked, "What were they wearing?" Within seconds, Lynn, using his law school savvy, asked, "What did the cop do then?"

"According to Ron, the Cat was wearing his baseball pants and a Stag T-shirt, and she was in her Bavarian outfit, but barefoot," Harold said. "Ron apologized for scaring them and told her to take the Cat home. Instead, she must have dropped him off at the ball park because Alton was supposed to play the first game this morning, and he didn't want to go back to Waterloo."

"Why didn't he sleep in the caboose or on the cemetery hill?" Lynn asked.

"He already knew some of our players might be doing that," Harold replied. "In case of rain last night, they were responsible for putting a tarp over the mound and home plate, and parts of the infield."

As the morning rain slackened, Lynn and Irish glanced again at the forlorn figure of a baseball manager in need of victory. Moments later, the roar of a tractor entering from a gate near the first base dugout caught the attention of those in or near the grandstand, and brought the Cat to an upright position.

"They'll disc the top soil on the infield, drag it, and be ready to go," Lynn told Irish as several Valmeyer players carried rakes to the home plate area and pitcher's mound.

After a two-hour delay, Alton completed its 2-1 victory over Clark Funeral Home. Cape Girardeau followed with a 3-2 elimination of the St. Louis Printers in what Lynn said was for "the Missouri championship."

Because of the low-scoring consolation games and clearing weather, ample time remained for the winners' bracket games pitting Millstadt vs. Waterloo, and the Champs vs. Valmeyer although the nightcap would bring more unique action.

Chapter 30

After the completion of the first two Saturday games, the Valmeyer tournament and its winners' bracket contests were sure to attract baseball fans. Meanwhile, the Champs relaxed before playing.

Worried about his players eating too much in the hot, humid weather, Red Morrison issued a warning but need not worry. Whether as grandstand observers of the rivalry between Waterloo and Millstadt or as listeners to baseball related stories, the Champs were about to receive food for thought.

"See the home plate umpire?" a male spectator sitting near Morrison asked. "He's a dandy," he said loudly enough for the Ashville contingent to hear.

With stacked beer cups, a pack of cigarettes, and a tourney program at his side, the grizzled fan told of the diminutive umpire he referred to as Willie making "the most famous call ever made here."

"Valmeyer was playing a St. Louis team last summer, and it looked like the Lakers were about to win after taking the lead on a long home run over the left-field foul pole," the fan said.

"When the ball left the park, it was hard to see if it was fair or foul, causing the St. Louis manager to rush toward home plate. When he got there, he towered over Willie and yelled, 'What did you call that?'"

"Everybody in the stands had heard Willie say, 'Fair.' But he has a speech impediment and stutters if he gets scared. So, when the manager asked again, Willie said, 'Fa-fa-fa-fa-fa-Foul!'

"Nobody from Valmeyer complained though. The ball was hit too high. Now, if there's a question, Willie holds onto his chest protector with one hand and signals fair or foul with his other hand."

Slightly amused, Morrison thanked the fan and moved closer to his team as home runs began to dominate the afternoon. First, Waterloo smashed five homers in a 9-6 victory over Millstadt. Three blasts by the losing team for a total of eight caused Mel Lynn to designate the day as "home run derby day in Valmeyer."

Influenced by the rash of four-baggers, Lynn reminded spectators at the second semifinal game that two pork steak dinners awaited the first batter to hit the caboose with a homer. In reality, the award was a secondary incentive for batters already enticed by outfield signs indicating just 295 feet from home plate in left field, 365 in center, and 305 in right.

For Slade, the afternoon brought attention to signs of a different type. Because of Morrison's powers of observation, the Ashville leader met his manager along the third base line after two Champs' batters had struck out.

What Morrison spotted may have been related to the Valmeyer catcher being tired from working on the diamond or from playing in 90-degree heat. Regardless, before every fastball, the catcher planted his right spike and twisted it into the dirt in an effort to become better prepared to receive the pitch.

Knowing what pitch to expect meant nothing unless Slade agreed, but Morrison knew his slugger had experienced something similar in 1953. That's when Slade told Randy Wilson of a Freeburg pitcher's tendency to kick his leg higher when delivering a fastball.

"I've got him," Morrison told Slade before giving his No. 3 batter a simple sign for whenever the manager anticipated a fastball. "If I clap my hands twice, it's a fastball," Morrison said.

Shortly thereafter, Slade tested the strategy by refusing to swing at a fastball in spite of Morrison's hand clapping. Fortunately, the same signal preceded the next pitch.

Swinging with all his might, Slade sent a high drive over the left-field fence and into the wall of a filling station some 100 feet beyond the road at the corner of the ballpark.

In the third inning, he became associated with another land mark when he shocked the bleacher creatures with a blast into left-centerfield and into a branch of an ancient oak tree. In the fifth inning, his two-run shot against the roof of the caboose was worth two dinners and a 4-2 lead.

"No telling how far it would have gone had it not been for the caboose," Lynn proclaimed. "Better check the ball to see if it's dented or if there's red paint on it."

Fearful of player misinterpretation, Morrison gave his hand-clapping signal only to Slade and Randy. The manager remembered all too well incorporating a verbal sign during his high school coaching days when saying "Forestall" meant suicide squeeze bunt. Used in reference to Navy Admiral James V. Forestall, who reportedly committed suicide in 1949, the signal was short-lived. Its death came after a batter missed the bunt sign and scorched a line drive past an approaching runner.

Against Valmeyer with Bob Range pitching well, the Champs prevailed until the eighth inning. By bunching two singles, two walks, and two infield errors, the Lakers tied the game and then took a 7-4 lead on a three-run home run by Kenny Meyer.

"Oh my! Goodbye! Home Run!" Irish chirped.

As the home town hero approached home plate, the roar of the crowd became so deafening that Lynn could have compared the clout to any smacked previously by a Laker, and no one would have heard.

"He'll dance tonight," Lynn said of Meyer, whose individual effort was overshadowed in the top of the ninth inning. With Valmeyer one out from victory, Slade, who had walked in the seventh inning, crushed his fourth home run in his fifth trip to the plate. The sizzling liner to left field cut the Champs' deficit to 7-5.

After another "Oh my!" by Irish, Lynn said, "You could hang laundry on that one."

Valmeyer manager Dennis Harold then took control by intentionally walking Wilson. When Ted Hill followed with a soft fly ball to center field, Valmeyer could aim for a title showdown with Waterloo. For the Champs, a game against Millstadt to decide third place lay ahead.

Reminded by Lynn to claim his home run dinners, Slade delayed his return to Ashville by offering the plates to Morrison and Walter Irish. As the manager and sports editor ate, the home run hero told them to take their time.

"Kathy and the kids are spending the weekend with her parents," he said.

On Sunday, in Valmeyer, the threesome would learn how baseball could contribute to more than sports page headlines.

Chapter 31

The trip to Valmeyer and the absence of a Sunday edition of the *Ashville News* gave Walter Irish and Joe Thompson an opportunity to exchange ideas related to the tournament and to the baseball activities in Ashville.

In addition to describing Slade's hitting exploits, which had tourney directors claiming the four home runs in one game were a first in the five years, Irish stressed why Valmeyer ranked high in the rich baseball history of southwestern Illinois.

"You should have seen what went on outside the right-field fence," Irish said. "There's so much room in the grassy area out there, a group of grade school kids were able to play baseball all day without bothering anyone."

"They ranged in age from about 7 to 13, and set up their own ball field by putting down what looked like potato sacks for bases and white towels for a pitching rubber and home plate. They followed their own rules because it looked like the pitchers threw slower to the younger kids and harder to the older ones.

"They only had one set of catching gear, and at the end of each inning, the catcher would put his shin guards, chest protector, and mask at home plate for the other team to use. Their baseballs were some of the foul balls Mel Lynn gave them from the men's games.

"They also had their own plate umpire. In place of real equipment, he used the lid of a metal trash can for protection like a regular ump using a hand-held chest protector. Whoever umped would peek over the trash can lid to call balls and strikes. Every now and then Mel and I would hear a loud ping from whenever a foul ball hit the metal lid."

Irish said he also peeked, but his was from the top of the dugout where he could observe the wives and girl friends of the Valmeyer players as they sun bathed in an area on the first base side.

"You bet I peeked," Irish said. "Some of them were as beautiful as Daisy Mae."

After expanding on the beauty of the July Fourth tourney visitor, Irish reminded Thompson of their schedules that would cause the sports editor to return to Ashville with Red Morrison and Slade.

"You can use my car again after the championship game, I'll ride home with Red and Frank," Irish said. "I'll write about the Champs against Millstadt for third place. You can cover the Waterloo-Valmeyer championship game, and add something on the Alton-Cape consolation game."

To please Irish, Thompson said he had written a story on the Muellers defeating Jasper Tile, 6-4, on Saturday. "I've got it here for you to take to the office in the morning," said Thompson before citing Les Mueller.

"He was wonderful," Thompson said. "He pitched well at the Athletic Field, and then became the talk of Saturday's activities at the Fairgrounds. After signing autographs, he went over to the ball throw stand and dunked Dutch Schmidt with one pitch."

Thompson also asked if teams other than the Champs took advantage of the open rosters at Valmeyer.

"As far as I know, Terry Plab and Randy Wilson are the only significant ones to this point," Irish said. "I've been told Waterloo has added Eddie Albrecht, and I wouldn't be surprised if he pitches for them today," Irish said.

"Who's Eddie Albrecht?" Thompson asked.

"He was born in St. Louis, lives in Cahokia (Illinois), and had a strange pro career," Irish said. "He's one of a few to win 30 games in a year. In 1949, he had a 29-12 record and 390 strikeouts in 330 innings for the Browns' Pine Bluff, Arkansas, team in the Cotton States League. That got him called up from Class C to the major leagues.

"With the Browns on the last day of the season, he won again. He allowed one hit – a triple against the White Sox. Because of rain, the game was stopped after five innings, and the Browns won 5-3.

"He may have hurt his arm in '49, but in '50 he was with the Browns at the start of the season. They were so bad their team president Bill DeWitt hired a psychologist to motivate them. The players said he used hypnosis, but that failed to keep Albrecht from being sent to the minors within three weeks. By 1954, he was out of pro ball."

Impressed with Irish's recall, Thompson asked if the sports editor knew of Roy Lee.

"He's the baseball coach at St. Louis U.," Irish said. "He pitched briefly for the Giants in '45 and has used his reputation to recruit players for the Collinsville team he has in the Ban Johnson League. He lives in Collinsville and has some of the best college-age players in the St. Louis area playing at Fletcher Field."

"How do you know about him?" Irish asked.

"He phoned the office yesterday and said he wanted some publicity on his team," Thompson said. "He made me feel like I should have known about Dave Nicholson, an outfielder who hit all kinds of long home runs last year and signed with Baltimore. Then he bragged about two of his infielders, and even spelled out and pronounced their names."

Aware of Dal Maxvill of Granite City and Jerry Buchek of St. Louis from a roster Lee submitted in early June, Irish responded with, "Maxvill without an 'e' at the end of his name, and Boo-check."

"Roy's a promoter, but those two guys are good," Irish said. "They got a lot of publicity when they were in high school and are two more examples of the talent on both sides of the river. If Roy calls again, tell him we can take his scores and highlights, but he can't be waiting several days before he gets something to us."

After giving the advice, Irish realized conversing with Thompson may have slowed their drive. Framed for the first time in the Chevy's side mirror was Morrison's 1950 Pontiac Streamliner station wagon.

"Do you think they talked about baseball?" Irish asked, referring to Morrison and Slade as the cars neared Valmeyer where the consolation game was underway.

Chapter 32

American poet Robert Frost once wrote: "Poets are like baseball pitchers. Both have their moments. The intervals are the tough things."

Had Frost referred to baseball managers rather than pitchers, his words could have been applied at Valmeyer where Alton's "Big Cat" cherished the moments. Ahead 6-2 in the fifth inning of the consolation game against Cape Girardeau, the manager was energized by a late-morning breeze and home runs. By the game's conclusion, a total of four home runs and an 8-2 victory meant he and his team had won two of three tourney games.

Presented the consolation plaque at home plate, the Cat reminded reporters of being as proud of the award as the two-game streak his team would take back to the Inter City League. Neither Joe Thompson nor other scribes reminded the manager of the triple play.

If home runs were a remedy for Alton, the same could not be said for the Champs. On the heels of hitting four consecutive home runs on Saturday, Slade added two homers on Sunday in a 4-2 loss to Millstadt and its knuckleball pitcher.

Unable to rely on signals from Red Morrison, Slade relied on the consistent swing he developed during his weekly routine with his Palooka batting tee. The first pitch he faced danced and darted, but he was able to lift the ball into left field where a steady breeze helped it clear the fence and land in the middle of the street.

After reaching on a base on balls in the fourth inning, he ignored his throbbing right knee in the sixth and accounted for the Champs' second run with another wind-aided homer. Although this one eluded the outstretched glove of the left fielder and traveled just over 300 feet, it did not keep Walter Irish from embellishment.

"Oh My! Goodbye!," Irish blurted. "That's No. 6!" he added without recognizing the decision he and Mel Lynn now faced.

"How the heck can we choose a Most Valuable Player?" Lynn asked after Slade had stroked his sixth homer to go with two doubles and 10 runs batted in.

Given the responsibility of selecting an MVP, the announcing duo resumed their discussion in the ninth inning when Slade walked.

"His only outs were those two fly balls in the first game," said Lynn. "Since then, he's reached base nine consecutive times with six homers and three walks. Overall, he's 8 for 10 and on base 11 times out of 13 trips to the plate."

Conscious of those numbers, Irish asked the obvious: "Can we give the MVP to a player whose team lost two of three games?"

"I've never heard of anything like that, but right now he's my choice," Lynn said. "If something dramatic happens in the championship game, we might find someone else, but no one else is close to those statistics."

Smart enough to keep the PA button off during their exchange, Lynn resumed "live" info after Randy Wilson lined out to the second baseman, and Millstadt had claimed a third-place plaque.

"They're another example of the best baseball in the Midwest," said Lynn, referring to Millstadt. He then reminded the growing crowd that the tourney MVP would be announced after the championship trophy presentation.

"Waterloo and Valmeyer for the title," Lynn said. "It doesn't get any better than exciting baseball and plenty of refreshments - wonderful ways to end a holiday weekend."

As Lynn took advantage of the decreasing wind to conveniently record the lineups for the final game, Irish used the time to mention other unusual award winners.

"Two years ago, at Notre Dame, Paul Hornung won the Heisman Trophy despite his team's 2-8 record." Irish said. "And in 1952, Bobby Shantz, a little left-hander, won the American League MVP while pitching for a fourth-place team."

Intrigued by Irish's comments, Lynn asked, "You telling me the Yankees won the World Series and didn't have an MVP?"

"Mantle and Berra had a lot of home runs and Allie Reynolds won 20 games, but Shantz was 24-7 for the Philadelphia Athletics," Irish said. He's with the Yankees this year, and listed at 5-foot-6 and 139 pounds."

"Too bad Slade isn't 5-6," Lynn said. "If he was short and hit six home runs, he'd be a shoo-in for most valuable."

"Too bad Albrecht isn't a Catholic priest," Irish countered. "If he stops Valmeyer, we could let the pitching priests share the MVP since Father Eichenseer and Father Hustedde won Waterloo's first two games."

Told to choose only one MVP, the announcers departed from conjecture and focused on the reality of Albrecht hurling a three-hitter and striking out 12 in a 3-1 championship victory.

"He used a go-to-hell curveball," Lynn told Irish of the former major leaguer's effort that calmed the Valmeyer bats but failed to quiet a spectator.

"If we'd had Morris Frank or Ray Rippelmeyer, it would have been a different story," the fan shouted of Frank, who won 22 games in the minor leagues with the Cardinals in 1949, and of Rippelmeyer, who reached the major leagues with the Washington Senators in 1962.

More concerned with the post tourney awards than hearing about two pro pitchers spawned in Valmeyer, Lynn proceeded. After recognizing the tourney winner and runner up, he recited Slade's game-by-game and total statistics before calling the third baseman by name and urging him to come to home plate to accept his award.

"Here's our MVP champion from the Champs," said Lynn, who drew applause that carried throughout the ballpark but had little impact on Slade.

Chapter 33

The conclusion of a holiday weekend and the Valmeyer tourney meant a return to normal activities for those involved in the festivities. Left for conversation until the next summer were the highlights of everything from a parade, fireworks, and live music and dancing to baseball and an unusual Most Valuable Player.

For the Champs, improvement became a necessity if the team intended to compete in the St. Clair Division of the Greater County League.

"You'll be okay," Walter Irish said in an effort to strike up conversation with Red Morrison and Slade as Morrison guided his station wagon out of the Borsch Park area toward Waterloo.

"We won one of three, but we were only outscored 12-11 in total runs," Morrison said.

"I thought Bauer and Smith were respectable in the last game," said Irish, referring to the pitching efforts of Tom Bauer and Ray Smith, who normally played outfield for the Champs.

Seated in the front seat, Irish may have thought the tap on his shoulder would lead to back-seat insight from Slade, but the sports editor quickly learned otherwise.

"Here, you can have this," said Slade as he handed Irish the MVP plaque. "You and Red both know I don't deserve it. Red gave me the fastball signals when I hit those four home runs against Valmeyer, and the wind was the reason for the last two against Millstadt. All I did was swing when I was supposed to and then got lucky."

"Bull crap," said Irish before failing in an attempt to hand the plaque back to Slade. "What's wrong with you?"

Greeted first by silence, Irish's question became the spark to a flame that ignited an explosion of explanation from Slade.

"Being MVP means nothing," Slade said. "The only thing I ever wanted was a chance to play pro ball. At least then I could have proved that I could succeed on my own."

"If I was good enough to sign, I could have found out just how good a player I was. I never got the opportunity. Sometimes I wonder if I kept playing because I loved the game, or because it was the only way to prove I should have been signed. You guys saw me in high school, and know I was better than some who signed."

Following more silence, Irish admitted hearing how some scouts thought Slade lacked what they called "the complete package."

"I guess that means run, hit, field, throw, and hit for power," Irish said. "But no one ever told me specifically why they didn't sign you. There were rumors somebody gave a scout a negative impression of you, and the word spread. I have no idea who 'somebody' was or if the rumor was true, but I've always had another hunch about you.

"I honestly believe there were so many players signed out of southwestern Illinois before the war, and so many in the minor leagues that you were overlooked. Then, after the war, you were in your 20s, and Major League organizations were signing younger players and guys who played pro ball prior to the war."

After driving past Waterloo and toward the western edge of Millstadt, Morrison may have thought otherwise, but his comment only added fuel to what bothered Slade.

"Don't kid yourself, Frank, you accomplished more in men's baseball than many who spent a year or two in pro ball and came home thinking they deserved more," Morrison said. "This plaque can make your wife and kids proud of you, and you won it facing some damn good competition."

Hearing the praise, Irish again offered the plaque. Again, Slade refused.

"From the time I was a kid, I dreamed of being Babe Ruth or Joe DiMaggio," Slade said.

"When I got older, I wanted to be like Stan Musial or some of the other Cardinals. At the brewery, when I listened to a game, if I heard Harry Caray describe an at-bat by Chuck Diering, I'd imagine myself in the batter's box instead of Diering. If I went to a game, I'd see me playing third base instead of whoever played there for the Cardinals.

"I read in *The Sporting News* how some players were signed on the basis of what scouts called 'potential.' That made it seem like a player didn't achieve as much as I did."

Turning again toward Slade, Irish offered two questions: "Are you any different than anybody else who didn't sign?" "What's the difference between you and Terry Plab?"

After hesitating, Slade replied.

"I don't know how other guys felt, but Plab was guaranteed a contract before his accident. All I ever wanted was a chance. I would have given anything to wear a pro uniform. And, if I had to be like the rookies Randy Wilson told me about, and forced to sit in front of the team bus to make sure the driver stayed awake, I would have done it."

Struck by the player's disappointment, Irish considered offering praise but failed when Slade continued.

"Maybe I should have done what you, Randy, and Johnny Champion wanted me to do in '53," he said, referring to the plan which had Slade replacing his look-alike Jim Dyck for an inning in a St. Louis Browns' game.

"The Browns are in Baltimore," said Irish. "There's no Bill Veeck to go along with a trick like that, and the Cardinals never would go for it."

As Morrison parked in Slade's driveway, the discussion came to an end.

"Don't make a big deal out of the MVP," said Slade before reluctantly taking the plaque from Irish and departing.

"Is this where Joe Palooka lives?" Morrison asked Irish, indicating that the Champs' manager was familiar with another Ashville rumor.

"Incredible story isn't it?" asked Irish, who felt compelled during the remainder of their drive to speak in confidence about Slade's reference to 1953 and the player switch with the Browns.

Chapter 34

In ancient Rome, the term "Dog Days" referred to the period from late July through late August. The Romans believed those hot days were associated with the star Sirius, which rose just before or at the same time as sunrise. Because Dog Days were considered an evil time, the Romans sacrificed a brown dog to appease the rage of Sirius, which caused the sea to boil and dogs to grow mad.

In the Greater County League, Slade and other players did not experience dog days of baseball when the mad blood could boil and a brawl erupt. By late July, the two-division league flourished with sportsmanship in accordance with Lee Mathews' desires.

Besides two GCL teams reaching the finals at Valmeyer, Slade, representing a third team, won the MVP honors. In addition, parity allowed several teams to contend for first place behind divisional leaders, Freeburg in the St. Clair and Waterloo in the Monroe.

At the all-star game at Scott Air Base where the St. Clair division defeated the Monroe Division, 6-3, Slade belted a single and a double in three at-bats. Terry Plab earned the MVP trophy by striking out seven of the nine batters he faced.

At the league meeting to announce postseason playoff procedures, Mathews also commented on the availability of American Legion players, including several yet to complete their high school careers.

"You can place any of these players on your roster, but you must remember they are committed to their Legion team first," Mathews said.

Support for Mathews' edict came in a Walter Irish column crediting the national American Legion program for developing outstanding current and former Major League players. Among the Legion graduates were Bob Feller, Stan Musial, Ted Williams, Yogi Berra, Warren Spahn, Frank Robinson, and Roy Campanella.

Irish quoted Musial as saying: "I was proud to wear the American Legion uniform because it was the first uniform I had."

According to Irish, in 1943, when Berra and his childhood friend, Joe Garagiola, were members of the St. Louis Stockholm Post 245 American Legion team, they both attended a Cardinals' tryout camp.

While Musial praised the American Legion for its contributions, Irish claimed the southwestern Illinois area featured several players whose potential had attracted pro scouts and led to tryout offers. Among those noted were pitchers Jerry Heintz, Ron Speiser, Norm Skikas, and Warren Ittner; catchers Ed Lange, Rich Sauget, and Mike Wittlich; infielders Chuck Hasenstab, Gordon "Moose" Meyer, Mike Hunter, and Charlie Webb, and outfielders Nelson Mathews, Kenny Meyer, Bob Toenjes, Larry Stahl, Bobby Price, Mel Patton, and Terry "T-Bone" Schwarz.

"This list may become incomplete as the summer moves along because more players will be recognized by coaches, managers, and scouts," Irish wrote.

If Irish influenced Lee Mathews, the sports editor was about to influence others with a meeting of his own at the *Ashville News*. His guests, Johnny Champion and Randy Wilson, were the same two he met with five years earlier. This time, his intent was to speak about what Slade referred to after the Valmeyer tournament.

"It's a reversal of how things went in 1953," Irish said. "You guys respected Frank and came to me with a plan for him to realize a dream by playing in a Browns' game, but he refused. He said those Sunday St. Clair League games, especially the playoffs, were his World Series games."

"Now, he's older, near the end of his baseball career, and very bitter. He didn't want to accept the Valmeyer MVP because he didn't think he earned it on his own. Now, he's saying he made a mistake in '53 and regrets not trying what you guys proposed.

"I reminded him about the Browns being in Baltimore, but the more I thought about it, I wondered if there's some way we can sneak him into a Cardinals' game, and he could be a pro player for a day."

Informed of Slade's change of heart, Johnny clasped his hands behind his head as if in deep thought, and then asked why Irish also would reconsider the idea.

"I'm for it because Frank represents more than a baseball player who never got the opportunity many others did," Irish said. "Look at you, Johnny, and at you, Randy, and at me. I'm the lucky one. I achieved my goals - being a sportswriter and editor, and getting to write a column.

"But not everybody reaches their goals. Johnny, are you comfortable being on your own as the heir to a sporting goods store? And Randy, aren't you upset with the loss of your parents and now being out of pro ball?

"How about Frank Slade? Maybe we can help him fulfill his dreams, and he can go on with his life without always wondering 'what if.' If our plan is foolish or too risky, we should have no regrets. Think about it, and if you come up with something, let me know."

Chapter 35

Although eliminated from all-star balloting because of not having played enough games with the Champs, Randy Wilson continued to contribute to the team's playoff hopes. More important was his desire to join Walter Irish and Johnny Champion for what the sports editor secretly called "Slade Day."

To Randy, offering a plan became a challenge. Each night as he tossed and turned, he fought frustration. Worse yet, was how, after he fell asleep, he encountered questions and dreams.

Was Irish's assessment accurate? Could Irish have any idea of how the former collegiate all-star envisioned playing in a Major League stadium as his parents watched? Could anyone understand how often he saw himself circling the bases after hitting a home run?

However, baseball was not the only subject to dominate his thoughts. Often, whether with a minor league team or more recently in Ashville, he recalled the night of his 21st birthday. The Champs, led by Slade's hitting, had won a game at the Southern Illinois Penitentiary and used Randy's birthday as reason to celebrate at each tavern stop en route to Ashville.

Hit on the left elbow (his throwing arm) by a pitch in his first at-bat in the prison, Randy eased the pain of his injury by downing Stag beer and snacks. Later, in Ashville, his medicinal remedy left him drowsy until he was awakened by a woman as beautiful as movie star Ava Gardner.

How enjoyable to recall her wearing a Baby Doll nightgown and standing in the doorway of his room with her firm figure silhouetted by light from the bathroom across the hall. How lucky to be greeted by a southern girl who said she arrived too late from Macon to disturb her Uncle Edward, but had retained a key to the store. How unfortunate to feel her caress and the touch of her hand across the cheeks of his face, only to awaken and realize she was gone.

Was there a link between baseball and the girl of his dreams? If so, Randy failed to appreciate a connection after waking from a dream in which he saw himself as an usher—first, at Busch Stadium in St. Louis, and then at the Georgia Champion theater. Was he like an usher and only able to watch a Major League game from the grandstands? Was he only an usher to Georgia and never a leading man?

Confused, Randy used the idle time of a Wednesday morning to approach Johnny with details of his dreams and inability to originate successful steps for Slade Day. At the store, they recalled when Randy stood at the front counter, pointed to an *Ashville News* photo of the St. Louis Browns third baseman Jim Dyck, and noted the striking resemblance to Slade,

"It would have been easy to make the switch then," Randy said. "Irish thought if Bill Veeck could put a midget in the batting order as he did a few years ago, he'd go along with a brief switch of players who looked alike. With the Browns gone and the Cardinals in control at Busch Stadium, we're stuck.

"Irish is still an official scorer, but there's no way he can come down from the press box and open the Cardinals' clubhouse door for what we want. We'd have to find someone to act like an Andy Frain usher to do that."

The words "Andy Frain" caused Johnny to quickly raise an index finger in an attempt to stop Randy's dialogue and exclaim, "That's it, Randy; Andy Frain's the answer."

"Don't you get it?" Johnny asked. "Your dreams were meant to help you solve our problem! Andy Frain ushers are at ball parks all across the country, and at places other than sports venues."

Continuing with recognition of the ushering service founded in Chicago in 1924, Johnny pointed to a framed photo of Edward Champion and a man dressed in a uniform and hat in military fashion.

"That was taken during a chance meeting at a sporting goods convention in Chicago," Johnny said. "Dad said he knew who it was after hearing one of the ushers say, 'Here comes the boss.'"

"After Dad introduced himself, a photographer took their picture, and, believe it or not, Mr. Frain mailed the photo here. Too bad it's in black and white. It doesn't show off the blue uniform with gold buttons and gold striped pants. Dad said the ushers all looked as classy as their boss.

"Whenever Dad showed someone the picture, he'd tell them of how Andy Frain ushers were so thorough one of them refused to admit Chicago Mayor Anton Cermak into the 1932 Democratic National Convention in Chicago. Apparently, the mayor didn't think he had to show a ticket. Dad also claimed Cermak has relatives living in the Ashville area."

In an attempt to resume deciphering his dreams, Randy reminded Johnny of trying to get Slade onto the field as a player and not as an usher.

"If we can put Frank into an Andy Frain uniform, we can get him into Busch Stadium," Johnny said. "Then, if we can get him into the Cardinals' clubhouse, he can change into a baseball uniform."

As Johnny returned to his desk, Randy paused and said, "It sounds too simple."

"We should talk with Irish," he said, causing Johnny to explain why he thought Irish became so supportive of Slade.

"He claimed otherwise, but he didn't reach all of his goals in life," Johnny said. "Before you came here in '53, everybody in town knew about his wife having an affair with an umpire in the St. Clair League."

"She was a teacher at the high school and a knockout, and somebody said after the end of the school year, she ran off with the guy. The ump was lucky because Irish bought a pistol at our store and wanted to kill the guy. When dad found out, he cooled Irish down, took the gun, and gave back his money.

"Irish never remarried, and that's why he's so devoted to his job. There's no doubt he lost something he loved."

Chapter 36

For Slade, the first Wednesday in August was no different than many other Wednesdays because of another Champs' practice. The difference on this particular hot, sultry evening emerged from a request by Red Morrison.

"We're coming down the home stretch of the season, and you've told me this will be the end of the line for you," Morrison reminded Slade.

"If you don't mind, at our last regular-season home game, I'd like to make some kind of gesture acknowledging you. You've been with the Champs every game since you came home from the war and been our leader."

Dressed in his usual dark blue sweat pants and gray T-shirt, Slade leaned against the first base dugout, looked at his manager, and posed a question.

"Red, are you doing this because of what I said after Valmeyer?" Slade asked. "I don't want anybody thinking I'm owed something."

"You're not owed anything or entitled to something," Morrison replied. "You've earned this. I've already spoken with Johnny Champion and the team, and they're in favor of anything we do for you."

Looking at the field as his teammates played catch, Slade said, "They're all good guys, Red, but I've got to talk this over with my wife."

Faced with that option, Slade added, "No Foul Ball for me tonight. I'll go home, talk to her, and get ready for work."

After thanking his manager, Slade joined the Champs. Later, as he prepared to leave the Athletic Field, he paused and reflected on quitting the game he loved.

"Why quit when I'm among the leading hitters in the league?" he asked himself. "Can my knee handle another year?" "Would Kathy complain if I changed my mind?"

Standing at home plate, he cast a shadow caused by the setting sun. Hesitating, he felt a chill while realizing his retirement as a player would mean leaving the place he called home since his high school days.

Was the baseball field bidding him farewell as he recalled the cheers of the 1953 championship game? Was the partial sunlight stretching like a beacon beyond the wooden, left-field fence a reminder of home runs hit high over the 330-foot sign? Was the circular Zephyr sign at the gasoline station across Illinois Street a reminder of his diminished power?

After all, according to Walter Irish, when Slade hit a shot that bounced in the street in front of the station, the homer became the second in distance to a blast by Negro League star Josh Gibson when the Athletic Field was known as Stag Park.

As Slade turned his attention to the right, he smiled and considered how many homers he would have hit had he been a left-handed batter.

Years of baseball brought visions of line drives and diving stops. In its silence, the Athletic Field allowed Slade to celebrate a career of which any athlete - amateur or pro, would have been proud. As he walked past the area once occupied by Edward Champion, he heard the applause of fans and hoped Kathy would approve Morrison's request.

For Morrison, more concern was about to surface at the sporting goods store where he had been urged to meet with Johnny Champion, Randy Wilson, and Irish.

Confident of gaining access to Busch Stadium, Johnny and Randy agreed they needed help for Slade Day to become a reality. Coincidentally, as the foursome gathered in the air conditioned comfort of Johnny's office, questions accompanied ideas.

Chapter 37

Accustomed to taking a leadership role after his dad's death, Johnny Champion felt comfortable in confiding in the three men he had called to his office. However, as he met with Randy Wilson, Walter Irish, and Red Morrison, Johnny had no idea of how an extraordinary plan would challenge his comfort.

Turning first toward Morrison, Johnny began with a reference to Slade.

"Red, you've known for years that Frank is plagued by not getting to sign a contract," Johnny said.

"Since he was a kid, he always did what he was supposed to do. In high school, he excelled in sports. But in baseball, his favorite sport, even though he was superior to others, the scouts ignored him.

"I've told Randy and Walter about your proposal for the last regular season game, and they agree it's a good idea. I also thought you should know what we're planning if Frank agrees with us."

Relaxed in the loft office where he often met with Edward Champion, Morrison quickly expressed his gratitude and said he expected Slade to accept anything, especially after hearing the veteran player express a change of heart.

"If he and his wife give me the okay, I'm going to get an engraved watch from Blanquart Jewelry and present it to him," Morrison said.

Curious about other plans for Slade, Morrison patiently listened to Johnny explain previous plans for the Champs' leader to replace his look-alike, Jim Dyck, in the St. Louis Browns' lineup.

"Time's running out," Johnny said. "I wish I could tell you we've got something that's as easy as walking next door to Blanquart's, but there's hope. After speaking with Walter earlier today, I think we both have great ideas, and you and Randy will be needed."

Nodding in agreement, Irish urged Johnny to continue.

"Tell him about the Andy Frain uniforms," said Irish, who had learned from Johnny how the uniforms could be incorporated on Slade Day.

"What does Andy Frain have to do with this?" Morrison asked.

"Randy and I will take care of that," Johnny said. "Be patient; what Walter told me today changed my mind."

"Do you really believe you can get him into a Cardinals' game?" Morrison asked.

"At first, we wanted to make him a Cardinal. Now, thanks to Walter and thanks to Cincinnati, we think we can get him into a Redlegs' uniform." Johnny said while pointing as an indication for the sports editor to continue.

"Believe it or not, Jim Dyck is back in the major leagues," Irish said. "He was traded from Baltimore to Cleveland to Cincinnati, and according to this week's *Sporting News*, he's been called up from the Redlegs' Pacific Coast League team."

"We need to get Frank into the Cincinnati clubhouse at Busch Stadium. And, just like our plan in '53, if we can detain Dyck long enough for Frank to get into a uniform and into a game for just an inning, we'll pull this off."

"Who told you Dyck will be in the lineup?" Morrison asked.

"It's just a hunch." Irish said. "Cincinnati will be in St. Louis for a doubleheader on Labor Day, and since both teams are out of the pennant race, I wouldn't be surprised if he's in there. If he's not listed, we sit back and enjoy the game."

"Aren't you guys afraid of being arrested or fined for something like this?" Morrison asked.

"What can they do to us?" Randy interjected.

"I saw people run onto minor league fields trying to get their hands on balls hit into foul territory and watched some woman jump onto the field and kiss our third base coach," he added. "The most the baseball chasers got was being kicked out of the park. I also read somewhere about a judge charging the woman with a misdemeanor."

Smiling at the thought of the woman, Irish reminded the group of their respect for Slade.

"We're here because we're willing to take a chance on something worthwhile," Irish said. "Let's take one thing at a time. I don't intend to approach Slade until we have everything in place."

"Count me in," Morrison said.

Pleased with the manager's decision, Johnny encouraged the group to keep everything confidential.

"Then tell me in confidence where the heck you intend to get Andy Frain uniforms," Randy said with a sense of urgency.

"Ask me tomorrow" said Johnny. "Remember, one thing at a time."

Chapter 38

When Walter Irish wrote "time is of the essence" in an August "Irish Brew," the sports editor was doing more than playing with words credited to English poet Geoffrey Chaucer. Time was of the essence for the fourth-place St. Louis Cardinals in their pennant chase. Similarly, for Irish and others involved with Slade being recognized or realizing a dream, time was diminishing.

By concluding with "time and tide wait for no man," Irish allowed readers to relate to the Cardinals without their knowing how he was extrapolating the expression.

Regarding time, Slade knew that only four days remained before he would stand at home plate at the Athletic Field and be the center of attention. At home after practice, he could not relay Red Morrision's request to Kathy because she and their children were at a downtown outdoor music concert.

Shortly after their return though, Slade was pleased to hear his wife say of the Champs' ceremony, "It's an honor we all can cherish."

"Our kids will be proud to stand at your side," she added.

Unsure of all the pre-game details and in a rush to get to work, Slade urged Kathy to phone Morrison and ask for specifics.

"He can tell you everything," said Slade before kissing his wife and telling their children he would see them in the morning.

As instructed, Kathy phoned Morrison and heard that Johnny Champion had arranged for a microphone and speakers at home plate.

"There will be chairs there for you, Frank, and your kids," Morrison said. "We've got an engraved watch for him, but we're not going to make a big production out of this.

"Johnny wants to speak on behalf of the team, and Frank will have his chance to say something. But we've also got a ball game against a good Tilden team. If we win, there's a possibility we'll be in the playoffs. If we lose, it could mean the end for Frank."

"What do you mean 'could'?" Kathy asked.

Sworn to secrecy about Slade Day, Morrison recognized his verbal slip and scrambled to correct his use of 'could.'

"You never know, Kathy, he might want to play in one of those pick-up games after the Greater County season is over," Morrison said. "The big thing now is the ceremony Sunday. Get there about a half hour before the game, and if I have more to tell you then, I will."

The manager's re-emphasis of Sunday allowed Kathy to extend her thanks, hang up the phone, and concentrate on guiding her children to bed. By the time she retired, she thought only briefly about Morrison's use of 'could,' and fell asleep wondering about what clothes she, her daughter, and sons would wear.

Across town, Johnny Champion continued to dwell on the importance of Andy Frain uniforms and the respect they generated. Alone in his living room near musical instruments, he resorted to methods used previously to clear his mind.

First, he strummed a few chords of "One Home Run" on his banjo. Then, he picked up his guitar and quietly sang lines from "Our National Pastime." After neither effort solved his dilemma, he sang the popular Italian love song "Volare" and stopped after the words, "where lovers enjoy peace of mind."

Thinking of his own peace of mind, he reached for a copy of the *St. Louis Post-Dispatch*. At times, reading helped him fall asleep. This time, one glance at the newspaper's front page accompanied an awakening that would carry over to the next day.

What drew his attention was a headline reading "Muny on Record Attendance Pace" and a three-column photo of the nation's largest outdoor theater with a seating capacity of 11,000 in Forest Park. Besides providing a panorama of the Muny, the photo showed an usher directing a patron to a seat location.

"That's it," Johnny shouted. "He's an Andy Frain usher, and that's where we'll get our uniform."

Had Johnny read the Page One story on the Muny, he would have known that St. Louis Municipal Opera attendance figures occasionally surpassed the number of fans watching a Cardinals' home game. Had he perused to the line reading, "President Eisenhower might be struggling with the United State economy, but there's nothing but the heights being hit at the Muny," he might have better appreciated the timing of the story.

"The Muny," he repeated as he turned out the living room lights. "The Muny!" "Why didn't I think of that sooner?"

Chapter 39

As momentum for recognition of Slade grew, the honoree was about to learn he was becoming the subject of a tale of two plans.

At home, late on a Thursday morning, he was awakened by "Yakety Yak," a song blaring from his daughter Kate's bedroom, and the chattering of his sons from a backyard swing set. Rubbing his eyes, he proceeded to the kitchen where he found his wife Kathy smiling.

Dressed in cut-off sweat pants and a T-shirt, Slade hesitated before realizing she was staring at his puffed, speckled hair.

"Must have been a heck of a game," he said, referring to his hair and another baseball dream.

After running his fingers across one side of his head in an attempt to smooth his appearance, he learned other reasons for Kathy's fixation.

"I told the kids this morning about Sunday, and they're excited," she said. "Red Morrison said we should be ready to sit with you near home plate. I'll make sure Jim and John wear shorts and nice shirts. Kate and I will wear summer dresses."

Appreciative of Kathy contacting Morrison, Slade explained the importance of the Sunday game - something he failed to do on Wednesday night before rushing off to work.

"From what I heard, we've got to beat Tilden, and the Muellers have to lose at Mascoutah for us to qualify for the playoffs," Slade said.

"We're tied for second place with the Muellers in the St. Clair Division behind Freeburg, and only the top two teams from each division advance to the playoffs, which start a week from Sunday."

More concerned with placing breakfast in front of her husband than with the outcome of the Sunday games, Kathy simply responded, "One day at a time."

"We've got other things than baseball to consider," she said while pointing to Ashville High School registration papers.

On this day though, Slade remained a topic as indicated by his sons' enthusiasm.

"Hey, Dad, you gonna be on a Wheaties box?" Jim asked.

"No, that's for guys like Bob Richards," Slade said of the Olympic pole vaulter gracing the cover of the boys' cereal box.

"If we collect enough box tops, why wouldn't they put your picture on a box?" John asked.

"Any pictures of me will have to show me looking well-dressed head to toe," Slade said with an emphasis on "toe" as a reminder for the boys to tend to their weekly chore of polishing their dad's spikes.

"The black shoe polish is where you put it outside in my gym bag," Slade said.

As the boys rushed to their assignment in a corner of the carport, a ringing telephone signaled more news for Slade.

"It's Mr. Morrison," said Kate, who had been the first to reach the telephone. After handing the phone to Slade, Kate moved toward her mother where the women could not be privy to a request by the Champs' manager.

"If you're willing to stick by what you said coming home from Valmeyer about playing in a big league game, just say yes," Morrison told Slade.

Without hesitation, Slade said, "Yes."

Morrison then told of a meeting that would include Johnny Champion and Randy Wilson.

"Tell Kathy you're going to meet with us and Irish tomorrow at the newspaper to learn more about being honored," Morrison said. "That way, you're not lying about anything."

"I'll be there by one," Slade said as he returned the phone to its kitchen wall location and then complied with Morrison's request.

"If there's anything I can do, just ask me," Kathy said.

"I'm sure you'll be included in everything," said Slade, knowing his wife eventually would have to be given the details of what could become another "Day" for her husband.

Chapter 40

Had Slade arrived prior to the 1 p.m. meeting at the *Ashville News*, he would have appreciated the dedication of Walter Irish, Red Morrison, Johnny Champion, and Randy Wilson.

After closing the sports section of the Friday *News*, Irish greeted the three visitors in a conference room where he hoped they could expand ideas broached on Wednesday night.

"Tell Red what you told me," Irish said to Johnny, who had phoned the sports editor that morning.

"Randy and I are going to the Muny Opera tomorrow night, and we've got a way to get an Andy Frain uniform," Johnny said.

"Why the Muny?" Morrison asked.

"Because I've been there, and it will be easier than trying to get a uniform at Busch Stadium," said Johnny.

Irish then offered advice for everyone involved. "If anyone of you considers this crazy, you better get out now," he said before re-emphasizing his "one thing at a time" suggestion.

"Red, at this point, we can't do a thing without an Andy Frain uniform," Irish continued.

"And, although we all may have thoughts on how to help Frank, we have to believe we're all going to contribute. You already did Wednesday when you agreed to help, and yesterday when you got him to confirm his willingness to go along with a plan.

"But I don't want anyone saying this is crazy. Crazy describes people like the woman who shot Eddie Waitkus in 1949."

With time to speak while waiting for Slade, Irish expanded on the story of the Major League first baseman shot in the chest by an infatuated female fan (Ruth Ann Steinhagen).

"Waitkus had been a star for the Chicago Cubs, but after the '48 season, he was traded to the Philadelphia Phillies," Irish said.

"When he was with the Cubs, the woman could control her obsession, but after the trade, she realized she'd only get to see him occasionally. One night in June, she lost control and checked into the Edgewater Beach Hotel in Chicago where the Phillies stayed. By leaving an urgent message at the front desk for Waitkus, she got him to come to her room. When he entered the room, she shot him with a rifle. He nearly died on the operating table before the bullet was removed from near his heart.

"What we're doing may not be an obsession for us, but it was for Frank and a lot of other guys who thought they were good enough to sign."

Within seconds of completing his rationale, Irish was interrupted by an intercom call from Joe Thompson in the sports department.

"Roy Lee's on the phone. He wants to talk to you about a hitting program he wants to publicize," Thompson said.

"Tell him I'll call him tomorrow," said Irish, whose irritated facial expression drew smiles from his guests.

Moments later, the group's attention turned to the arrival of Slade, who was about to hear matters Irish had not discussed with anyone.

"Frank, since you're willing to go along with our scheme, you have to understand getting you into a Cincinnati uniform is not going to be easy," Irish said.

"I've been thinking of our various roles, and if Johnny and Randy come up with an Andy Frain uniform, we should be able to get you into the Redlegs' clubhouse. All you'll have to do is change into a uniform and be ready to bat in place of Jim Dyck at the start of the second game of the doubleheader.

"The problem will be finding a way to get Dyck out of the ballpark long enough for you to take his place. Getting an usher's uniform comes first. After that, I've got ideas. For now, let's relax and enjoy Slade Day at the Athletic Field on Sunday."

Irish again emphasized the importance of secrecy and scheduled another meeting for Wednesday night at the Foul Ball.

"For all we know, you might be in the playoffs," Irish said to Morrison. "Regardless if you practice on Wednesday, by then we should have more to consider and be ready to move forward."

"Any questions?" Irish asked.

"Do you guys really believe you can pull this off?" Slade asked. "Aren't there big risks?"

"We've discussed that, and as long as we all respect your regrets related to pro ball, we're willing to give it a try," Irish said.

When no other question followed, the group departed as Johnny directed a type of theatrical expression at Randy, saying, "Let's break a leg tomorrow."

Realizing Slade overheard the comment, Johnny added, "Don't take that literally on Sunday, Frank."

Chapter 41

On June 16, 1919, *Robin Hood* was the first show performed under "The Muny" banner at the St. Louis Municipal Opera in Forest Park.

How ironic that the first municipally-owned outdoor theater in America to host the heroic outlaw of English folklore would greet men intent on robbery on the night of Saturday, August 9, 1958. In this case, unlike Robin and his band of merry musicians reveling on stage, Johnny Champion and Randy Wilson would perform backstage.

"This shouldn't be difficult," Johnny said as he steered his Lincoln Capri into the Muny parking lot. At ease after that comment, Randy also enjoyed hearing that Mary Ann Jerome, the daughter of Ashville Mayor Jacob Jerome, would sing the national anthem prior to the start of the evening's production.

"Without her, we'd be stuck wouldn't we?" Randy asked after being reminded that as an eighth-grader, Mary Ann had sung the anthem on Homecoming Day in 1953 at the Ashville Fairgrounds.

"She's in college now and has been involved with the Muny since she was one of the children in a scene from *The Wizard of Oz*," Johnny said. "Being the daughter of a mayor has some clout, but she's an excellent singer. Too bad they're doing *Rose Marie* instead of *Damn Yankees*. If Slade liked Damn *Yankees*, you'd like it too."

As the Ashville pair approached the Muny entrance, Randy admitted he knew nothing of the musical *Rose Marie* and turned his attention to an Andy Frain usher.

"Don't worry about him," Johnny said. "Mrs. Jerome told me to show our tickets and then go to our right where she'd meet us at the top of the steps."

After gaining admission, Johnny led Randy to a pergola type walkway on a side of the theater where an usher stepped aside for Mrs. Jerome.

"Excellent timing," she told Johnny, who introduced Randy to Mrs. Jerome and reminded them of the Homecoming Day when Mary Ann performed prior to a skit featuring the ball player.

"Johnny told me he's been here with his McKendree theater group, but never backstage," Mrs. Jerome said. "After Mary Ann sings the anthem, you both can meet us during the overture."

In the backstage area, which was nearly as wide as the 50-yard outdoor stage, Mrs. Jerome led Johnny and Randy to her daughter. A striking brunette, she sat behind a mirrored table in a corner of the room. Dressed in white blouse, navy blue skirt, and black leather pumps, she appeared as professional as the lead performers entering and exiting nearby dressing rooms.

After expressing pleasure with their invite, the visitors toured the dressing rooms and "change shacks" constructed near the stage entrance for quick wardrobe changes. On the ground level of the Muny, Mrs. Jerome pointed to administrative offices, restrooms, and other rooms, including one whose open door exposed ushers' uniforms and hats.

"That's where the ushers can put on a uniform or change into their street clothes after a production," Mrs. Jerome said. "Years ago, there were showers down here so anyone could freshen up."

After returning backstage, Johnny said he and Randy would meet the Jeromes during the overture and then would return to their seat locations at the end of a row on the east side of the Muny.

"That will work because just before the music ends, Mary Ann and I will go out the opposite door to our seats on the west side," Mrs. Jerome said.

Once the "Merry Men of Slade Day" were seated, Randy received instructions.

"When we go backstage, tell the Jeromes you need to use a restroom downstairs," Johnny said.

"An overture can last as long as five minutes, and that should be enough time for you to put a uniform into a bag. We can't wait until intermission. There will be too many people backstage."

As Mary Ann sang the anthem, Johnny stood at attention with hand over heart and observed other patrons. Several rows in front of him, an elderly woman, dressed in an expensive, flowery, silk dress, used opera glasses to attain a better view of the singer. At her side, a male patron wearing a flashy, seersucker suit, closed his eyes and silently lipped words from the anthem.

The song's conclusion brought an ovation for Mary Ann, who exited from the west corner of the stage while Johnny and Randy eased through a door on the east side. At the rear of the backstage area and away from performers anxious for the production, the thieves again met the Jeromes.

"Your voice is beautiful," Johnny told Mary Ann. "It's so good, I'll bet you're better than the woman performing 'Indian Love Call,' tonight."

As Randy excused himself according to plan, Johnny engaged in conversation related to his being able to identify the signature song of Jeannette MacDonald and Nelson Eddy in Broadway productions of *Rose Marie*. As the overture continued, Mrs. Jerome pointed to a brief biography of her daughter in the evening's published program.

"She's going to be a sophomore at Northwestern University," Mrs. Jerome said. "Maybe the day will come when she's singing and acting here."

Hearing a familiar part of the overture, the mother and daughter stood and began their departure from backstage. After bidding farewell, Johnny turned to find an approaching usher carrying a brown paper bag.

"How do I look?" asked Randy, whose entry into a vacant ushers' room had allowed him to don an Andy Frain uniform.

"Let's get out of here," Johnny said as he grabbed the bag and led their exit to a side of the Muny and past their seat locations.

As the overture concluded, they encountered an approaching usher on the top level of the pergola side.

"Where are you guys going?" he asked, causing Randy to step in front of Johnny and respond.

"I've got to get this guy to the parking lot," Randy said. "He's sick."

Were it not for the dim lighting at the rear of the Muny, the suspicious usher might have noticed Randy's dark brown shoes worn in violation of a Frain rule requiring men and women ushers to wear black shoes.

"Get back here before intermission," the usher said to Randy, who responded with a nod, a grasp of Johnny's right arm, and an increase in their pace. By the time they reached Johnny's car, *Rose Marie* was in full production. The same could be said of the efforts in support of Slade.

"Good thing you didn't grab the uniform of the Canadian mounted police," said Johnny, who used the time en route to Ashville to provide a synopsis of the musical. As Johnny punctuated the drive with repeated singing of "I am calling you" from "Indian Love Call," Randy placed his Andy Frain hat and tie into the brown bag with his other clothing.

Chapter 42

Within a day of leaving *Rose Marie* and its emphasis on love, Johnny Champion and Randy Wilson attended another love fest on Sunday afternoon at the Athletic Field in Ashville.

As Slade appropriately stood in the batter's box, he was surrounded by Kathy, their three children, and the Ashville Champs. Already saluted by Walter Irish in the Saturday *Ashville News*, Slade humbly accepted the adulation of everyone from Ashville mayor Jacob Jerome, to Johnny Champion, to Lee Mathews, to Red Morrison.

According to the Champs' manager, Slade led the Champs before and after his Army service.

"He played with pride and showed the type of class all baseball players should display—regardless of the level," Morrison said.

Before handing the honoree an engraved gold watch, Morrison said, "This watch is a token of our appreciation. It reads, 'To: Frank Slade, The Champion of the Champs, August 10, 1958.'"

Applause then broke out from home plate to the first base side where the Tilden Merchants gathered in front of their dugout to the grandstands where a crowd of nearly 300 spectators cheered.

Given an opportunity to use the microphone whose black chord extended to the grandstand where an announcer's booth once existed, Slade expressed thanks to his family, those preceding him with the microphone, his teammates, and the Tilden team. Next, he pointed to Walter Irish, who stood aside Joe Thompson near the ballpark's entrance.

"Mr. Irish, you've followed me since I was a high school kid and written many things about me," Slade said.

"You've always been fair and accurate through victory or defeat, health or injury, and as a player, I can't thank you enough. Some people may wonder why I never signed a professional contract, but I wonder why the *New York Times* or *The Sporting News* didn't seek someone with your skills."

That praise drew a nod of thanks from Irish, who was applauded by spectators aware of the sports editor's tribute to Slade in the *News*.

"Hopefully, you will have much more to write about after today's game," Slade concluded.

As the teams prepared for the first pitch of the game that could determine if it would mark the end for Slade, Irish turned toward Thompson, who cited Slade's character.

"He's as classy as what you indicated yesterday," said Thompson in recognition of a "Brew" in which Irish highlighted Slade's high school and men's league achievements.

In part, Irish wrote: "Many baseball players have been developed in the southwestern Illinois area. Some reached the major leagues, but only a few maintained a love of the game equal to what Frank Slade has displayed.

"Had he signed out of high school as an all-state third baseman with impressive statistics, he may or may not have advanced in pro ball. Yet, there's more to him than numbers. In his way, he's been a major leaguer for a long time."

To avoid an overemphasis on statistics, Irish labeled Slade "a power hitter and all-star," prior to describing home runs that landed on the porch of a home across from the Athletic Field.

"He hit that left-field target as a teenager and thereafter," Irish wrote before dwelling on diving stops, leaping catches, strong throws, and then emphasizing the 1953 Champs.

"That team had Randy Wilson, who was recruited by the late Edward Champion, but without Slade as a mentor, the kid from Indiana might not have reached the pros."

Of the final game of the '53 playoffs, Irish referred to Wilson tagging up at third base and scoring the decisive run against Freeburg after the catch of a fly ball off the bat of Johnny Champion.

"That was memorable, but after Wilson singled, he could not have advanced without Slade following with a shot off the third baseman's glove," Irish wrote. "Slade was held to a single, but it was inches from being a game-deciding double to the left-field corner."

Alongside the Irish column was a photo not used in '53 in deference to one showing Wilson sliding home beneath a catcher's glove.

"Examine the photo," Irish urged readers. "That's Frank Slade holding Johnny Champion high in the air. On Sunday, we all will have an opportunity to give high respect to Slade."

Regardless if influenced by Irish or Thompson's story identifying the Champs' need for a victory, spectators stood and applauded in unison as Slade approached the batter's box for his first at-bat. By then, Slade Day in Ashville already was a success.

Chapter 43

I f being honored prior to the game placed pressure on Slade, his first at-bat against Tilden pitcher Dave Luechtefeld brought increased anxiety.

An all-state basketball player at Okawville High School, the 6-foot-7, 225-pound Luechtefeld once scored 52 points in a game during his senior year. Also a fast-balling, right-handed pitcher, he expanded his talent and earned an athletic scholarship to St. Louis U.

According to Joe Thompson (in a Saturday story), Luechtefeld was like 6-foot-8 Gene Conley, who pitched for the world champion Milwaukee Braves and also played pro basketball for the champion Boston Celtics. Recruited by Tom Kirk, Luechtefeld was used sparingly in the Greater County League because he also pitched for Roy Lee in Collinsville.

"More scouts will see you if you're playing against men," Kirk had told Luechtefeld.

With Tilden out of contention for the St. Clair Division playoffs, Luechtefeld stood tall in a spoiler's role. Against the Champs, he struck out the first two batters in the presence of St. Louis Cardinals scout Walter Shannon, who had been contacted by Kirk.

Had Shannon been seated with Johnny Champion and Slade's family behind the home plate screen, the scout would have been no less conspicuous than from his front row seat in the grandstands.

Because of word of mouth, he signed autographs for youngsters, but as Slade approached the batter's box, the scout resumed writing into a notebook.

Luechtefeld's size and the speed of his fastball made him a can't-miss pro prospect, but the game of baseball can demand more. Those qualities surfaced after Slade and Randy Wilson received base on balls due to pitches well out of the strike zone.

After the two-out walks, Luechtefeld seemed headed out of danger when Vernon Koester bounced a ground ball toward the second baseman. Although Koester was slow afoot - like many catchers, he reached first base as the ball rolled beneath the infielder's legs and into right field.

Because Slade and Randy ran on the three-ball, two-strike count, their base running accounted for a 2-0 lead. As Slade raced home from second base, Randy sprinted toward third base and was sent home after the right fielder's throw to third sailed out of play.

As if by script, the Champs remained ahead in the fifth inning when another infield error and a dropped fly ball in the outfield set up Slade for a heroic opportunity. Retired on an infield pop-up in the third inning, he hit a rocket off the left-field wall. As he slid into third base with a triple, fans applauded the Champs' first hit of the game and a 4-0 lead.

When Randy followed with a looping single just over the shortstop's head, Slade scored to support pitcher Bob Range, who allowed three runs in the late innings. Luechtefeld, who yielded five hits, struck out 15 but walked nine.

Range, in contrast, struck out five and scattered nine hits while relying on his defense. Among the key plays was a diving catch by Slade, whose throw to first base completed an eighth-inning double play.

Because the 5-3 victory did not clinch a playoff spot, most of the Champs remained near their third base dugout after the game. Meanwhile, Slade moved toward his family in the grandstands where the persons waiting to greet him included Shannon.

"You're a hell of a ball player," the scout said loudly enough for Slade's family, Johnny Champion, and Walter Irish to hear.

Looking directly into Shannon's eyes, Slade extended his right hand for a lengthy handshake, but said nothing. In a gesture that seemed to show he understood, Shannon placed his left hand over Slade's right hand and held it there until the veteran player spoke.

"That kid's a hell of a pitcher," said Slade as he withdrew from the handshake.

If Shannon had intended to say more, he failed to do so because of the appearance of Thompson running with hands held high through the entrance of the Athletic Field.

"Muellers lose 4-1; Champs make the playoffs!" he yelled.

"Looks like they'll be playing at Freeburg next Sunday," said Irish, who heard from Thompson how the pitching of Terry Plab and clutch hitting by Mascoutah center fielder Jim Albrecht stopped the visiting Muellers.

As players and spectators walked past the journalists, Irish reminded his reporter of their responsibilities.

"We've got to inform our readers of the significance of what went on here today and the importance of all the games," he said, knowing he continued to face the challenges of another Frank Slade Day.

Chapter 44

I n many ways, Frank Slade Day at the Athletic Field did not mean the end of his being recognized for an outstanding baseball career.

Readers of the Monday *Ashville News,* for instance, were treated to a sports page photo of Slade accepting the watch from Red Morrision. Slade's daughter Kate was so impressed, she sought copies of the three-column picture for placement in a scrapbook and on the walls of her and her brothers' bedrooms.

On Wednesday afternoon in downtown Ashville, the desk of sports editor Walter Irish featured another copy of the recent photo. Torn from the first page of Monday's sports section, the photo of Slade, his family, and dignitaries was heavily circled in black ink.

Alone in the second-floor office, Irish sat at his desk and held an envelope and letter that accompanied the sports page. After placing the envelope postmarked "St. Louis, Mo., PM, Aug. 12, 1958," on top of the torn page, he read for a third time the letter's typed contents.

Dated August 11, 1958, it began with a salutation and parenthetical comment of: "Dear Mr. Irish (I use the term Mr. loosely)," that foreshadowed the letter's tone.

"Enough is enough! First on Saturday you resurrect a photo from 1953 to honor the Great Frank Slade and then you do it again on Monday with that crap from before Sunday's game.

"Did you sell more papers because of that? Or was it all part of your love for Slade who you felt was the player that the pro baseball scouts missed?

"Slade's an amateur and you're an amateur. You're like Slade! You've both been stuck in Ashville because you weren't good enough for the Big Time. For him it was baseball and for you it was not being hired by the *St. Louis Globe* or *Post-Dispatch*.

"I guess because the Champs have reached the playoff, you're gonna be happy with more time to kiss Slade's ass."

Signed "A Reader Smarter Than you," the letter concluded with: "P.S., Show me some guts and publish this letter!"

"Kiss my ass!" Irish mumbled before shoving the torn sports page aside and placing the letter in the middle of his desk. After taking a red marker from the desk drawer, he proceeded to circle punctuation, spelling, and capitalization errors, and circle where punctuation was omitted.

"You're either a dumb SOB or trying to trick me," he thought as he placed commas where needed and then put a diagonal line through the G in Great to indicate a lower case letter. When he finished, the letter looked like it had suffered a case of measles, and continued to bother Irish.

"Why typed?" he asked. "If someone was smart enough to use a typewriter, wouldn't they punctuate better?

"Why the St. Louis postmark?" "Were they actually from St. Louis, or were they from Ashville and trying to hide?" "If the person who wrote it refused to sign it, why not just place it in the drop box near the entrance to the newspaper?"

"Was this done out of jealousy or hate?" he repeatedly asked himself. "Was it from a man or a woman, an opposing player, a teammate, or just a know-it-all reader? Was this the person who misinformed the scouts when Slade was in high school? What did they know about me and the *Globe Democrat* or *Post-Dispatch*? Was this another case of 'somebody said'?"

Proud to be associated with the *Ashville News* from when he started out of high school as a young reporter, Irish found security in the late

1940s when he became the sports editor and was encouraged to write a column.

"I didn't apply for a job across the river," he told himself. "If they wanted me, I might have jumped at an increase in pay, but driving to St. Louis didn't appeal to me."

Ironically, he often spent time in St. Louis during the Cardinals' seasons when he shared official scoring duties with Ellis Veech, the sports editor of the *East St. Louis Journal*.

"What's so bad about publicizing the men's league when the Cardinals are on a road trip to San Francisco and Los Angeles?" Irish asked himself. "These guys deserve as much space as anybody on a sub-.500 Major League team."

Glancing at the letter again, he returned it to its envelope and then tore everything into pieces and deposited them with the accompanying sports page into a waste paper basket.

Assuming the writer a man, Irish asked himself, "Wouldn't this guy shit if he knew about another Slade Day?"

Despite being pitched from "Letter to the Editor" consideration, the anonymous letter carried enough clout to increase Irish's resolve to aid Slade. As Joe Thompson entered the office, Irish, with phone in hand, already was urging Johnny Champion to attend a meeting that night at the Foul Ball.

Chapter 45

Walter Irish was not the only Ashville recipient of a Wednesday surprise. As the sports editor stewed over the anonymous letter, Slade received a shock when he opened his mail box. Inside, with a letter from Ashville High School, bills, and a woman's magazine, was a note taped to a 10-ounce, glass bottle.

After placing the mail on the kitchen table, Slade separated the handwritten message from the bottle and read: "Dear Frank, Congratulations on your career. Here's something to help you finish like a race horse entering the home stretch. Best Regards, Terry Plab."

Pushing the note aside, Slade took the bottle in hand and read the remnants of its labels: "Horse Liniment. Sore Muscle and Joint Relief. Soothes Arthritis. For external use on Livestock only." Turning the bottle around, he found the following advice: "Avoid Contact With Eyes. If you rub, don't wrap. Wash hands thoroughly."

Curious about the bottle's contents, Slade gently twisted its cap but quickly closed it because of the resulting smell.

"Is this a joke, or is he sincere?" he asked himself before recalling the pitcher's injury. "No one who suffered like he did would joke," he concluded.

Recalling how he had spoken of his tender right knee in conversation with Plab at Valmeyer, Slade became confident of his appraisal. With Mascoutah out of the playoffs, the gesture seemed genuine.

Once again, he opened the bottle and wrinkled his nose as he sniffed the liniment.

"Who knows?" he asked himself as he placed the bottle and the note into the bag he would carry to what would be his last Champs' practice if the team lost on Sunday.

At the Athletic Field, he refrained from telling Red Morrison of the liniment, and displayed an intense desire to lead the Champs.

"We've beaten Freeburg before, and we can beat them again," Slade said to Morrison.

"You look like a kid again," Morrison said after several line drives.

"Just lucky," Slade responded.

Urged by Irish to remind Slade and Randy Wilson of the meeting at the Foul Ball, Morrison told Slade, "He's not calling it to interview us about the playoffs."

At the Foul Ball, Irish complimented Johnny Champion for contributing to earlier plans for the second Frank Slade Day and also revealed increased intensity to move forward. After detailing new plans and a time frame for all involved, Irish surprised his listeners by saying their circle of secrecy would grow.

"Frank, you've got to tell your wife," Irish said. "Just as in the case of last Sunday at the Athletic Field, if she's opposed, we can stop the whole thing. There's a playoff game this Sunday, but even if you keep winning, the finals will be over before Labor Day. That's when Frank Slade, the pro, will appear.

"If she agrees, she'll have to convince your kids they're going with you to watch the Cardinals and Cincinnati. They don't need to know the real reason for going to the doubleheader."

That night, Slade smiled as he watched filled Stag beer bottles pass his station. By then, Kathy, after being informed of the plan and its designers, had said, "Yes."

Chapter 46

I f the anonymous letter writer sought the worst for Walter Irish and Slade, the writer should have enjoyed reading the Monday, August 18, *Ashville News* sports section.

A "Freeburg Rips Champs" headline confirmed that Slade had been on the losing side of the St. Clair Division playoff game. From a journalistic standpoint, Irish also was a loser as a result of a headline over a wire service story from Los Angeles.

"Cards, Dodgers Spit" was a nightmare for an editor. Major leaguers do spit, but "Split" properly would have meant each team winning a game in their doubleheader.

Against the Champs, Freeburg rode the pitching of Clyde Pruett and hitting of Lloyd Schanz, a strapping left-handed hitter whose two home runs sparked a 7-1 romp. After one of the homers landed on a school bus parking garage in deep right field, Irish asked observers if the blast was the longest ever at Freeburg.

With no definitive response, he turned his attention to Pruett, a crafty right-hander who contrasted with the hard-throwing efforts of Ronnie Warren in previous playoffs.

"Clyde Pruett was Michelangelo as he painted a classy four-hitter for the ages," Irish wrote of the pitching choice of manager Austin Mulkey. "If the Champs were prepared for fastballs, they became baffled by Pruett's soft-toss accuracy."

According to Morrison, "He could have thrown curves through the eye of a needle."

After stressing that Pruett walked none and had errorless defense, Irish wrote in how-they-scored fashion. The latter allowed him to account for the Champs' scoring on a sixth-inning double by Randy Wilson, who also singled twice.

Slade's name did not appear until the ninth paragraph where mention of the game being played in an open park served as likely ammunition for the anonymous writer.

"Denied a home run in the third inning because of the left fielder's deep positioning and catch, Slade went 1-for-4 with a single to center field in the ninth inning," Irish wrote.

After saluting Slade a week earlier, Irish use a brief sentence to link the end of the player's career with the Champs' elimination. He also limited his reference to Waterloo's 5-2 victory over Valmeyer in the Monroe Division because of Joe Thompson's account of that game.

As Irish sat at his office desk, he re-read Thompson's story and a line crediting "the heavenly tosses" of Father Ed Hustedde for Waterloo.

"How could I miss the hyperbole and use spit instead of split?" Irish asked.

Returning his attention to the Cardinals' story and box scores, he tried to minimize his errors by criticizing the lead paragraphs of an Associated Press story from Los Angeles.

"The Cards break a four-game losing streak with a 12-7 win in the first game of a doubleheader, but the AP goes nuts over four hits by Stan Musial," Irish thought. "What about Curt Flood and Gene Freese beginning the game with back-to-back home runs off Sandy Koufax?"

After reading how the 22-year-old Koufax took a 9-5 record into the game but did not get through the second inning, Irish dug into the box score to confirm the Dodgers' use of veteran pitcher Carl Erskine for five innings in a mop-up role.

Slightly soothed by his critique, Irish found added comfort when he looked at a calendar opposite his desk.

"Back in the saddle tomorrow night," he thought, referring to Busch Stadium where the Cardinals would open a 16-game home stand against Philadelphia.

Checking the schedule again, he realized the home stretch would end on Labor Day weekend.

"Better not be any screw ups on Labor Day," he told himself as his thoughts bounced from writing and editing to Slade.

Chapter 47

Being eliminated from the Greater County League playoffs did not mean Slade had finished playing baseball. Another Slade Day remained, meaning he could have an opportunity to become a pro ball player, and might get one more chance to bat.

As Labor Day approached, Slade and others involved with the plan headed by Walter Irish faced more than the challenge of secrecy. For Slade, preparations included trying to maintain some semblance of his hitting ability, especially after a rip in the side of Joe Palooka's head had kayoed the carport punching bag.

As a result, Slade resorted to using lunch-hour time at the brewery to take practice swings in a corner of a loading dock. Fortunately, other employees already were accustomed to watching him establish a stance, stare at an imaginary pitcher, and swing through the air.

Had the workers been closer, they could have heard Slade murmur, "Here's the pitch" prior to each swing.

"Let him alone," said one observer to another. "He's just doing what he's always done and is still upset about never getting signed."

Had Irish heard about Slade's lunch-hour swings, he might have objected because readers of the *Ashville News* should have known the Champs had lost. Meanwhile, by assigning Joe Thompson to the August 24 Waterloo at Freeburg game to determine the first playoff championship of the Greater County League, Irish could concentrate on the Cardinals.

Secure with his plan, the sports editor knew there would be nothing he could do to assist Slade if Jim Dyck was not in the Cincinnati lineup. Another conflict arose after Birdie Tebbetts resigned as the Redlegs manager in mid-August and was replaced by Jimmy Dykes, a fact Irish recognized in a column.

"Harry Caray will have fun if manager Jimmy Dykes (pronounced dikes - like dike with an s) puts Jim Dyck (pronounced dike) in a game" Irish wrote.

"Regardless of who plays," Irish continued, "the Redlegs need someone to support the hitting of Frank Robinson if they are going to put a finger into the dike that would stop their recent flood of losses."

If the reference to Dyck or play on words evolved from desire to assist Slade, Irish felt justified because Dyck played previously in St. Louis - with the Browns.

"He was among the Browns' leaders in 1952 and '53 and deserves recognition," Irish wrote.

Information from press corps members of teams visiting St. Louis also fed Irish's obsession. According to two Philadelphia writers, Dyck saw limited action against the Phillies, but started the second game of a doubleheader and batted third.

If similar occurred in St. Louis, and Dyck did what other major leaguers occasionally did during the first game of a doubleheader, Irish could celebrate and share a dream with Slade.

"As this season winds to a close, the Cardinals and Redlegs must work on Labor Day if they intend to reach the .500 mark," Irish noted. "They'll need labor and luck to succeed."

Only those involved with Frank Slade Day could fully appreciate the meaning of his conclusion.

Chapter 48

Despite assurances from Walter Irish, Slade carried doubts about the plan to sneak him into a Major League game.

Rain may have postponed the Greater County League playoff finals to August 31, but nothing slowed Slade's anxiety. Whether as a spectator with Red Morrison at Freeburg where the host team defeated Waterloo, 6-2, or en route to Ashville, Slade offered what ifs.

"What if I get caught before I get on the field?" Slade asked. "What if someone else fails to do what they're supposed to do?"

"Just do what Irish told you, and the rest will fall in place," said Morrison, who would begin his part in the plan by picking up Slade on Labor Day and driving to St. Louis.

On the morning of the holiday, Slade's wife Kathy contributed to the secrecy by telling her children their grandfather William "Bill" Ellis had six tickets for the Cardinals' doubleheader and wanted to drive the family to Busch Stadium. Given an opportunity to impress, especially after refusing to attend the previous Slade Day, Ellis enjoyed the deception related to the tickets. In reality, they were purchased by Kathy through Irish.

Told earlier in the week that their dad and Morrison received two Cardinals' tickets, the Slade children had no reason to question why their dad declined accompanying the family, including Mrs. Ellis.

Two hours after Ellis' departure, Slade, wearing slacks, a red T-shirt, and black loafers, looked like any other baseball fan headed for Busch Stadium, except for the red gym bag he took to the passenger side of Morrison's station wagon.

Leaving Ashville after the start of the doubleheader allowed Morrison to tune into the Cardinals' radio broadcast. As the Champs' manager and Slade approached the Eads Bridge and the Mississippi River, the Cards held a 1-0 lead on a second-inning, RBI single by Wally Moon.

"We gonna make it on time?" Slade asked.

"Right on schedule," said Morrison while Harry Caray moaned about Vinegar Bend Mizell walking another Cincinnati batter in a duel against fellow lefty Joe Nuxhall.

After reaching Dodier Street, one of the streets alongside Busch Stadium, Morrison told Slade to remove a wooden barricade at the entrance to the Home Plate, a restaurant located across the street from the first base side of the stadium. In the parking lot at the rear of the restaurant, Johnny Champion stood near his Lincoln Capri with two men wearing blue military style outfits trimmed in gold.

"Since when did you become an usher?" Slade asked Dutch Schmidt, who laughed as he stood next to Randy Wilson.

"Anything to help you," said Schmidt, making it obvious the original circle for the Slade Day had grown.

As the group entered the back door of Home Plate, Slade wondered what other surprises lay ahead. After being directed to a corner table, his apprehension was tempered by the restaurant owner.

"I'm Anthony Bonelli," he said. "If you guys are the ones Walter Irish told me to expect, just sit here and relax while we wait for the end of the first game."

Accustomed to greeting everyone from Cardinals' fans to sportswriters to Major League players before and after games, Bonelli supported a reputation built on excellent pasta and baseball conversation. On this occasion, the Ashville visitors formed the bulk of his audience as Caray's voice, from a shelf-top radio behind the bar, held listeners.

"If Mizell pulls this off, he might set a record for most base on balls in a 1-0 shutout," Caray said.

Hearing that the game had reached the ninth inning, Champion reviewed each step in Irish's plan. Shortly thereafter, Randy and Schmidt returned to the parking lot where they donned the rest of their Andy Frain outfits while Champion, Morrison, and Slade remained inside.

From their vantage point as they listened to Caray's game-closing comments with fellow broadcasters Jack Buck and Joe Garagiola, the Ashville trio could see through the restaurant's picture window and across the street. Conspicuous on that side of the stadium was a narrow, metal door marked "No Entrance."

After Caray repeated the particulars of Mizell's four-hitter, featuring nine walks and just one strikeout, Buck said the shutout was the first for the Cardinals since July 24. Of greater interest to the Home Plate group was watching Jim Dyck emerge from the metal door and walk past Schmidt, who represented the bulkiest of Andy Frain ushers.

By the time the Cincinnati third baseman entered the restaurant, Slade had exited through the back door although not without observing his look-alike. Similar in height, weight and age, the dark-haired Dyck was more of a double for Slade because the latter had changed his hair color from speckled to dark black.

"Need a sandwich between games?" Bonelli asked Dyck as the casually dressed player took a seat at the bar while observing the other two customers.

"Anything will be an improvement over what they have in the clubhouse," Dyck replied. "I ate better and got paid more in the Pacific Coast League."

After telling Bonelli that he (Dyck) was allowed to watch the first game from the grandstands, the player said he was in no hurry to return because Max Patkin would be performing.

"I've seen his act, and he's the reason we won't have infield practice before the second game," Dyck said.

On cue with the Irish plan, Champion and Morrison moved from their table to the bar where Dyck was bombarded by the strangers' enthusiasm.

"I saw you play for the Browns, and you were damn good," Morrison said.

"Are you happy with Cincinnati?" Champion asked.

After having his ego stroked, Dyck refrained from taking a bite of his sandwich or a drink from a Coca-Cola bottle in deference to responding.

"You guys sound like you really follow baseball," was a reply that lengthened the conversation and allowed Bonelli to discreetly place a "Closed" sign in a corner of the picture window.

"Baseball's a funny game," Dyck said before referring to the joys and sorrows he experienced after being drafted by the Browns from the New York Yankees in 1948.

As Dyck expanded on his comments, Patkin brought cheers from the Busch Stadium spectators without knowing his antics would be needed to assist Slade.

Chapter 49

Upon entering through the metal door on the Dodier Street side of Busch Stadium, Slade could hear fans cheering Max Patkin. The Clown Prince of Baseball, Patkin put to use his rubbery long neck, toothless face, askew ball cap, and baggy uniform, which displayed a question mark rather than a number on his back.

Good enough to earn a brief minor league career as a pitcher, the skinny, 6-foot-2 Patkin claimed he began his clown career in 1944 when he was pitching for a Navy team in Honolulu. After giving up a home run to Joe DiMaggio, Patkin left the pitcher's mound and followed the renowned slugger around the bases.

On the field at Busch Stadium, Patkin looked more like a dancing Gooney bird than a batter getting a hit. Meanwhile, beneath the steel beams of the grandstands, Slade measured his steps and walked briskly to the Cincinnati clubhouse where he met Randy Wilson.

Dressed in an usher's uniform and seated on a folding chair, Randy quickly guided Slade into the clubhouse. "Money talks," Randy said, referring to the deceit of Walter Irish. Able to enter the stadium because of his appearance, Randy was equally successful in replacing Gus "Doggie" Russo, the longtime visitors' clubhouse attendant.

After being handed two small, manila envelopes, Russo opened one labeled "Doggie" and found two $5 dollar bills paper clipped to a note written on Cardinals' stationery. The note read: "Doggie, sorry for disturbing you. Please keep the enclosed because it is imperative that you deliver the second envelope to Ellis Veech, the official scorer in the press box. He also may have a reward for you."

Despite the note's scribbled closing, the letters BD in script were discernible enough for Russo to whisper, "Bing Devine." Thinking the initials belonged to the Cardinals' general manager, Russo told Randy to remain outside the clubhouse and permit only Cincinnati players or Patkin to enter.

After entering the clubhouse, Slade found a locker marked Jim Dyck, undressed, and changed into the major leaguer's uniform. Taking his spikes and glove from the red gym bag, Slade then placed his street clothes into the bag and handed it to Randy.

"So this is what a big league clubhouse looks like," Slade told Randy after observing ham and cheese sandwiches on a table and a hamper filled with soiled T-shirts, socks, and towels.

More prominent in a corner of the room was a desk where a nameplate indicating "Dykes" identified the desk as belonging to the Cincinnati manager. Among the items on the desk was a radio whose volume was low but loud enough for Slade to hear Harry Caray say, "Once Patkin gets off the field, we should be ready to go."

That pre-game comment sent Slade to Randy, who agreed it was time for the new Jim Dyck to enter the Redlegs' dugout. Walking cautiously down the narrow runway leading to the home plate corner of the dugout, Slade stepped aside for Patkin, whose inquisitive stare was more shocking than his words.

"Go get 'em Jim," Patkin said.

After making no response, Slade felt extra apprehension when he read the Redlegs' batting order taped to the wall at the dugout entrance. Printed in black ink were last names and numbered positions starting with Temple 4, Lynch 9, and Dyck 5, representing the first three batters and second base, right field, and third base, respectively.

By having Dyck bat third, Cincinnati contributed to Irish's plan since Slade would be guaranteed an at-bat in the first inning.

Taking a seat near the bat rack in the dugout, Slade realized he and the bat boy were alone because Jimmy Dykes had moved to the middle of the dugout to put a halt to some of the players trying to duplicate Patkin's facial contortions. Already in a grouchy mood, the 61-year-old Dykes grumbled upon seeing Slade.

"Where have you been?" Dykes asked.

"Took a crap in the clubhouse," Slade said.

"Well, at least you weren't out here jacking around with these guys," the manager responded.

Also a former major leaguer, Dykes was accustomed to the freedom he had granted Dyck and showed no suspicion as Temple entered the batter's box. After accepting a Jim Dyck model bat from the bat boy, Slade glanced at the Cardinals' lineup that was minus Stan Musial but kept MVP candidate Ken Boyer at third base.

On the mound stood Jim Brosnan, a 6-foot-4, 210-pound, bespectacled right-hander, whom the Cardinals obtained in May in a trade with the Cubs for infielder Al Dark. By coincidence, Brosnan was the winning pitcher when the Cubs shut out St. Louis in the teams' 1958 season opener. Signed by Chicago at age 17, Brosnan won 17 games on the Class D level in 1946 to become a highly-touted prospect.

With the Cardinals, he again showed flashes of brilliance by striking out Johnny Temple on three pitches and retiring Jerry Lynch on a check-swing grounder that brought Slade to the plate. In his 11th season in pro ball, Brosnan wondered if he had ever opposed former American Leaguer Dyck.

As Slade established his stance, only he and a few of the 15,155 spectators knew that the pitcher had never faced this batter.

Chapter 50

Whn Slade dug into the Busch Stadium batter's box, he had multiple reasons for failing to relax. Brosnan was imposing from 60 feet, 6 inches, and from a closer distance, Cardinals' catcher Hobie Landrith posed a threat.

By singing "The stars at night," the first four words of the song "Deep In the Heart of Texas," Landrith hinted at being in the Class AAA Texas League with Jim Dyck. Told by plate umpire Tony Venzon, a native of Thurber, Texas, "to knock it off," Landrith laughed and attacked Slade's nerves by referring to the batter's shoes.

"Those sure are pretty," Landrith said. "Get those in the Texas League?"

"Got 'em in the Pacific Coast League," said Slade, who suddenly realized his shoes were the only non-Major League item of his Jim Dyck apparel.

As Brosnan fired a fastball for strike one, Landrith may have relished his chatter. Slade, though, was only following the plan meant for him to savor every second of his at-bat. According to Irish, Slade could take pitches until being called out on strikes or swing away whenever he wanted. Under no circumstances was he to take a base on balls and increase the chances of being discovered.

After Venzon called a second fastball a strike, Slade knew he must seize the opportunity to hit or walk back to the dugout and out of the stadium with nothing more than brief memories. Although he was not intimidated by the Busch Stadium atmosphere, he found Brosnan's pitches superior to any others he had seen.

Either the result of Brosnan's guile or Landrith's desire for variety, the third pitch was a curveball. Thrown at a reduced speed and hanging in the strike zone like a balloon on a windless day, the ball allowed Slade to take a full swing and hit the pitch to right centerfield. Fortunately for Slade, the ball rolled to the base of the outfield wall, meaning he would not have to stop at first base with a single and come under the scrutiny of first baseman Joe Cunningham or first base coach Tom Ferrick.

Whether motivated by the fear of being caught or assisted by the horse liniment he applied to his right knee that morning, Slade sprinted for second base. As he approached the bag, he knew he would have to beat the throw of right fielder Wally Moon.

With the crowd caught in anticipation, Slade prepared to slide as Cardinals' shortstop Eddie Kasko reached for Moon's throw on the outfield side of second base. By sliding at the inside portion of the bag, Slade avoided Kasko's tag and drew a call of "Safe!" from umpire Frank Secory before an incredible chain of events.

Because of his hard slide, Slade could not stop his momentum and failed to retain possession of the bag. From a supine position, he reached back with his right hand and was inches from the base when Kasko made a swiping tag, knocking Slade's cap off his head.

"Out!" yelled Secory, who became as curious as Kasko at the sight of what appeared to be black cream or polish on the shortstop's glove.

"What in the hell!" Kasko screamed as Slade retrieved his cap and the baseball that Kasko had shaken from his glove while examining the black residue. If Kasko had acquired a memento, Slade had another. With ball in hand, he sprinted toward the Cincinnati dugout as Kasko trailed in hot pursuit.

Given another opportunity to look ahead of himself while running, Slade was stunned as he viewed the grandstands where his wife, children, and in-laws stood and cheered.

"He's got the damn ball!" Kasko shouted as the intensity of the events multiplied.

From the broadcast booth to every level of the stadium, all eyes were on the field where the play should have concluded the first half of the inning.

"Damndest thing I've ever seen," Harry Caray said of the umpire's changed call at second base.

After listening to Caray on the Cincinnati clubhouse radio, Max Patkin seized the opportunity for recognition and returned to the Redlegs' dugout. As Slade approached, Patkin charged past him and onto the field where he might have collided with the charging Kasko had it not been for the shortstop skidding to a sudden halt.

Directly in front of Kasko were the suntanned legs of a female spectator, who sat on the concrete wall separating the box seats from the playing field.

"I haven't seen legs like that since I saw Ava Gardner with Frank Sinatra in Los Angeles," Jack Buck told listeners.

On the field, Patkin became the center of attention by sliding into second base and then approaching a stunned Secory. After extending both hands as if to signal "safe," the clown raised the thumb of his right hand into the air as if to indicate "out." As both teams delayed coming onto or off the field, the crowd cheered.

Meanwhile, as an Andy Frain usher escorted the Ava Gardner look-alike from the box seat area, a male spectator wearing black slacks and a white shirt stepped from his grandstand seat and onto the Cincinnati dugout. Once there, he placed a foam rubber replica of a redbird on his head.

After walking and then hopping from end to end of the dugout, the animated bird beckoned to a female spectator. Dressed in a bright red blouse and black skirt, the enthusiastic fan joined the bird for a dance shortened by Patkin's arrival.

"Get out of here while you can," Patkin said after gliding between the youthful partners and initiating leg kicks to the delight of the crowd.

Also encouraged by an usher to leave, the dancing pair departed just before Patkin took a deep bow and stepped off the dugout. Pleased with the importance of his performance, he was not surprised in the dugout where he stepped aside to allow the real Jim Dyck to move quickly toward third base.

"Baseball's a funny game," Garagiola said as Venzon urged, "Play ball!"

Chapter 51

Unable to hold onto second base during his slide, Slade reached a home plate of sorts in subsequent actions. After changing clothes in the Cincinnati clubhouse, he sped through the Dodier Street exit and headed for the Home Plate restaurant. As he entered, he was oblivious to the sign Anthony Bonelli changed to "Open" shortly after Jim Dyck had sprinted across the street.

Delayed by compliments and questions from Red Morrison and Johnny Champion, Dyck lost more time when he encountered Dutch Schmidt outside the player entrance to the stadium.

"Can't you read?" asked Schmidt, whose Andy Frain outfit and gruff voice forced Dyck to seek entry at a regular stadium entrance.

Slowed again by an usher seeking proof of an admission ticket, Dyck yelled that he was a ball player and needed to get into uniform for the second game of the doubleheader. Only by grabbing a scorecard from a nearby vendor and pointing to his name on the Cincinnati roster was he able to enter.

When he reached the clubhouse, he confronted another usher in the form of Randy Wilson. By then, Randy had led the gym bag-carrying Slade to the street entrance. Recognizing Dyck, Randy pushed the clubhouse door open and told the player to hurry. Time also became a matter for Randy when he heard from a distance the command of Doggie Russo.

"Stay right there, young fella!" Russo shouted.

Thinking it best to remain at the clubhouse door rather than causing a commotion by sprinting to an exit, Randy sat in anticipation.

"Any problems while I was gone?" Russo asked.

"Had to escort two women and a male spectator out of the grandstands," Randy replied.

"Good job; get back to your other station," said Russo, whose return was delayed by the note delivered to scorekeeper Ellis Veech.

Typed on Cardinals' stationery, the brief, unsigned note read: "Ellis, thanks for all you do."

Pleased, the East St. Louis sports editor showed the note to Walter Irish. Unaware of the note Russo had received, Veech returned to his duties as the clubhouse attendant observed the press box atmosphere.

After watching Slade on the field and witnessing Russo's presence in the press box, Irish became convinced his plan had been successful. However, he acquired few facts because of his journalistic duties and the progress of the game eventually won 9-3 by Cincinnati.

At the Home Plate, as participants in the plan gathered at a corner table, they knew that Irish had insisted on secrecy but learned there had been a stretch to the silence. In addition to Slade, Johnny Champion, and Morrison, the Slade Day group included Schmidt, Randy Wilson, Georgia Champion, Joe Thompson, and a female, introduced only as "Miss Redbird" by Thompson.

"Heck of a job," Johnny told Morrison. "You knew more St. Louis Browns' players than Dyck did."

"Mr. Bonelli did as much as me," said Morrison before telling the group that Irish often frequented the restaurant before and after games.

"Everybody was great," Slade said.

"How'd you get involved?" Johnny asked Thompson.

"Best not to tell the boss he hasn't mastered turning off the intercom at the *News*." Thompson said. "When I heard about the second Slade Day, I thought I'd go to the Cardinals' doubleheader and help out if needed."

"Ingenious," Randy told Thompson.

"Couldn't have done it without her," Thompson said while pointing to the accomplice he had met as a dancing partner on the second day of the Valmeyer tournament.

"What would we do without women?" Thompson asked while turning his attention to Georgia Champion.

"Nothing like having a loyal cousin," Johnny explained. "And don't forget Frank's wife," he added.

Although eager to compliment Kathy Slade for getting her children and Bill Ellis and his wife to the game, Johnny stopped speaking when he saw Ellis approaching the group.

"Hey, Frank," said Ellis as he tossed the keys for his Cadillac to his son-in-law. "There's a car full of proud folks wanting you to drive them home."

After catching the keys, Slade accepted Ellis's handshake and reminded Morrison about the red gym bag in the car of the Champs' manager.

"Looks like the parade starts here," Slade said, not knowing Grand Avenue was about to host a line of cars, including a Cadillac, a Lincoln Capri, a Pontiac station wagon, a red Rambler American, and a Ford convertible displaying Georgia license plates.

After arriving at the Slade residence, the drivers left the driveway entrance to the carport open for a 1952 Chevrolet belonging to Irish. As the group awaited his arrival, there was no surprise in the seating arrangement that placed Randy and Georgia side by side as were Joe Thompson and his guest.

During conversation ranging from recall of Slade's at-bat to Randy's theft of two Andy Frain uniforms at the Muny to Thompson's redbird, Irish appeared. His arrival signaled the placement of a large white cake and ice cream on a table.

Atop the cake, written in red icing was: "Congrats, Frank, Always a Pro."

"I guess you all know how much today means to me," Slade said while holding his wife close to him. "Sometimes we do get what we wish for."

"You earned it," Irish said. "And, I don't believe Jim Dyck is going to tell anybody about you."

"Max Patkin won't either," Thompson added.

Not far from the lighthearted discourse, Kate Slade drew a lingering smile from her dad.

As daughter and dad watched the Slade twins play catch with a new baseball in the back yard, she asked, "Is that another kind of double play?"